Enjoy This Complimentary Copy
From The Author!
www.ANovelByCornellGraham.com

THE OTHER SHOE DROPPED

To: Frances
Enjoy!

Cornell
2/25/08

Other Novels By Cornell Graham

- *Prophet Priest & King*
- *A Bitter Pill To Swallow*

THE OTHER SHOE DROPPED

A Novel

CORNELL GRAHAM

www.ANovelByCornellGraham.com

The Other Shoe Dropped is a work of fiction. The characters, incidents and dialogue are the results of the author's imagination and are not to be construed as actual. Any references to real products, events and/or locales are intended only to give the fiction a sense of authenticity.

The Other Shoe Dropped is a novel by Cornell Graham

Book & Cover Design By Cornell Graham
Front Cover Photograph By Cornell Graham
Author Photograph By Cornell Graham

First Printing: February 2005
ISBN: 0-9715949-2-9
Library of Congress Control Number: 2004093703

Please address questions, feedback and any requests for additional copies to:
CORNELL GRAHAM
P.O. Box 2364
Alpharetta, GA 30023

Email: scrg400@att.net / Web: www.ANovelByCornellGraham.com

Printed in the United States by Morris Publishing, Kearney, NE 68847

Dedicated To My Niece

Latrice White

There is no wisdom, no insight, no plan
that can succeed against the Lord.
The horse is made ready for the day of battle,
but victory rests with the Lord.

Proverbs 21:30-31

ACKNOWLEDGEMENTS

Without a doubt it is by the power, mercy and grace of my Father that I publish this third novel. Thank you once again, dear God, for all your blessings – both seen and unseen.

As always, thanks to my family for their continued support of my efforts – Debra, Zachary and Kristyna.

Thanks to the following for their continued media support: INK Newspaper in Fort Wayne, Indiana; ADVERTISING AGE magazine; BOOKING MATTERS magazine in Atlanta; and Deborah Godwin Starks' radio program in Fort Wayne, Indiana.

Thanks to Ravonne Green, Library Director at BRENAU UNIVERSITY in Gainesville, Georiga for inviting me to speak to students about my works.

Thanks to the various book clubs that choose my works as one of their book club selections – with special thanks to *Second Saturday Book Club* and *Women of Essence Book Club* in the Atlanta area.

Thanks to the bookstores across the country as well as online retailers that make my books available. Special thanks to Debbie Pitre of HIDDEN TALENT and to Denise O'Connor of BARNES & NOBLE in Norcross, Georgia.

And last, but not least, thanks so much to my loyal readers as well as new readers, especially those of you whom I've had the pleasure of meeting on the golf course. Your support is greatly appreciated. Please feel free to provide me with feedback at any opportunity. May God bless you always!

THE OTHER SHOE DROPPED

CHAPTER
ONE

The silver Buick Park Avenue became swallowed into a sea of noon hour traffic as it merged haphazardly onto Interstate-75/85. The bumper-to-bumper congestion crawled forward in the summer's heat like a herd of cattle. The impatience of many drivers equaled that of children in a candy store. Tempers seem to flare at the blink of an eye.

His thick sweaty hands were nearly strangling the steering wheel as he feverishly fought his way into the I-85 northbound lanes that would hopefully escort him out of this mess.

The air conditioning system in his fourteen year-old car had already surrendered its last breath of coolness sometime back in June when the temperature outside had reached ninety-plus degrees. To fix the darn thing would have cost him more than what the car was worth. So, he chose to endure the never-ending suffering. Although, on this searing Tuesday in mid-August, as the mercury inched towards one hundred, he began to second-guess his decision to put up with this routine madness.

A few miles ahead the traffic picked up, and so did the speeds. Several vehicles raced past him like there was no tomorrow. And perhaps there wasn't. Maybe *today* was *the* day that business needed to be taken care of. While he had absolutely no clue who the faceless drivers were that zoomed past him one by one, oddly enough, he understood their need for such speed. Maybe they, too, had *important* matters that

2 / CORNELL GRAHAM

had to be taken care of with a sense of urgency. Who was he to judge them? It was simply a sign of the times – people had to be seen; places had to be gotten to; deals had to be closed.

For him, however, there had been a long awaited score to settle – a wrong to right.

He stole a peek into his rearview mirror. For just a moment an eerie feeling enveloped his unassuming, dark bulky frame as he attempted to discern the pair of cue ball eyes staring back at him. He tried, to no avail, to remember the precise point in time when he'd allowed himself to become this *different* person. This individual who didn't seem to care anymore – about anything nor anyone. He was an aging man who found himself, lately, acting more on emotion rather than reason.

He wasn't proud of who he'd suddenly become.

Irrational. Irreparable. Irrepressible. Such words had come to describe his demeanor quite easily. Could he really be so uncompassionate? So heartless? So brutal?

Somewhat ashamed, he averted his gaze from the rearview mirror and stared ahead, his eyes wandering across the interstate toward nothing in particular.

It was apparent to him that he'd been driven to the edge. Or, perhaps even *pushed*.

His left hand gripped the steering wheel tighter as his right one was suddenly given a reprieve, but not before he brushed the hand against the leg of his denim trousers to remove an accumulation of sweat. The heat and humidity inside the car was almost unbearable as he began scratching the top of his head, his fingers sinking into a thick wool of hair. He was in desperate need of a haircut. Even though the Afro seemed to be making a stylish comeback, he had no desire to lug around a bunch of hair again. It was pure neglect that allowed it to grow this long in the first place. Besides, at sixty years of age, he didn't think that it looked appropriate for him to have that much hair. Especially since, as a landscaper, he spent a majority of his time outdoors in Atlanta's sweltering heat. The style had once been appropriate for him, but that was back in the sixties and seventies. Now, he was quite content to leave the Afro look to those hip-hop-music-listening, sagging-jeans-wearing teenagers, as well as those video music rappers he occasionally watched on BET.

He resumed driving with both hands firmly holding the wheel. Another glance into the rearview mirror was stolen. His eyes had become even more haunting. Part of him wished that things didn't have to be handled this way, but he realized that it was too late to turn back.

Slowly, he shook his head as he tried to understand the *foreigner* in the mirror. The man's physical features were undeniably his. It was with the man's soul that he found himself wrestling so vehemently.

Then suddenly, like the rising of the morning sun, it dawned upon him. It was *they* who had changed him. *They* who had repeatedly ignored his telephone calls. *They* who had refused his many requests to meet with them privately. *They* whose ears had become dull and unwilling to listen. It was a totally irresponsible way for *them* to conduct business – a business that they obviously had no idea how to run.

Their father never would have treated him with such disdain. Such utter contempt.

The gentle welling of his eyes, and the subsequent blurring of Atlanta's skyline through the rearview mirror as he drove farther north, made him realize just how much he missed the late Everson Alexander. The man was a business and creative genius. His untimely death, one year ago today, had rocked Atlanta's advertising community like a major earthquake, and the aftershocks were yet to subside.

He recalled the first time that he'd met the then middle-aged Everson Alexander twelve years ago in 1992. A small diner just outside of the Sandy Springs suburb in Atlanta was where the two men would eventually strike hands in pledge. It turned out to be a successful meeting. Two African-American businessmen coming together and working together for a mutual benefit. Everson had been managing his newly formed ad agency from his home at the time, so he often met clients or potential clients at their place of business or some quaint restaurant around town.

It was his landscaping business that became the first client to join the ALEXANDER AGENCY. Everson had promised to create an image and advertising campaign for him that would make the business stand miles apart from his competitors. Everson had also promised to help him attract more business from the commercial sector as well.

And did he ever deliver on his promises!

Thanks to some creative newspaper ads and catchy radio spots from Everson's agency, his landscaping business grew rapidly. His advertising spending eventually increased from a few thousand dollars per year to well over $3 million. Everson personally handled his account until the day he died. And although Everson's ad agency itself grew quickly, billing more than $125 million annually, the man never treated him any differently, despite having much larger clients that demanded a lot more of his time. But Everson Alexander had been the sort of man to make each client feel important – large or small. Admittedly, over the years he certainly enjoyed being treated like a big fish among Everson's prestigious clientele, and not as if he was just some irrelevant minnow.

Irrelevant. That was how they had described his account now.

I'm sorry sir, but we're just too large and too busy to handle an itty-bitty client like you. Please feel free to give us a call when you're ready to spend . . . say ten million or more.

His lips pursed with suppressed fury. They didn't even have the audacity to drop him from their client roster face to face. Instead, they chose to do their dastardly deed by U.S. Mail – the mail for Pete's sake! Was he not worthy of a FEDEX delivered letter? Or, how about a hand delivered notice by a local messenger?

Oh, he would make them pay dearly for their cowardly actions!

A swerving pick-up truck nearly ran him off the road as he exited I-85 and entered onto the ramp leading towards Georgia Highway 400. He gritted his teeth but decided to remain calm. Obviously, it was just another faceless driver with some important business to tend to.

His hands were now drenched in perspiration as he reached over and patted the black leather attaché case that lay on the passenger seat. An affected grin formed across his beefy face. "We're almost there," he muttered to himself. His smile grew incriminating as he allowed himself to visualize the terror on their pretty little faces when he took control of the situation.

After dispensing fifty-cents into the wide-mouth bucket to pay for the toll and then waiting patiently for the gate's arm to raise and let him pass through, he sped along towards the Perimeter Mall area. The red needle on the Buick's speedometer quietly approached seventy before he took notice of it. He eased his size-ten sneaker from the accelerator until the needle hovered between fifty-eight and sixty. He didn't want to risk being pulled over by some ambitious cop trying to make his ticket quota. Not today. That would definitely throw a monkey wrench into his carefully laid plans – especially if they decided to search his attaché case. That course of action would prove to be disastrous, to say the least.

He was quite comfortable with this less conspicuous driving speed. In due time he'd arrive at his destination. He was certain of that. After all, there were two people that needed to be seen. A distinct place in which he needed to be. Something of the utmost importance that needed to be done.

If it was the last thing he ever did in his entire life, he was going to see to it that it got *done* – today.

CHAPTER TWO

When the LAST WILL & TESTAMENT of EVERSON JAMES ALEXANDER was read, one week after his burial, no one was more stunned than Milan and Paris Alexander, his twin daughters. The subdued proceedings had taken place high above downtown Atlanta within the offices of Everson's attorney, Blade Barnes. It had been revealed that the two women would not only inherit their father's multi-million dollar ad agency, but that they would also assume and share equal control of its day-to-day operations – all at the mere age of twenty-five. The bittersweet declaration made Milan and Paris the youngest co-CEOs of a multi-million dollar advertising agency, one that ranked within the top ten among Atlanta's ad firms.

The soft-spoken Milan had been teaching fifth graders at the time of her father's death. Her desire and love for teaching was realized when, as a junior in high school, she had the opportunity to serve as a mentor for some disadvantaged students within the public schools system in Atlanta. While she'd always admired her father's hard work and his many accomplishments with the agency, she had never seriously considered following in his footsteps. Instead, the field of education had become her pursuit. She earned a *B.A.* degree in *Child Development* from SPELMAN COLLEGE.

Her sister, on the other hand, never had college on her radar screen, much to the disapproval of their father. The feisty and often outspoken Paris was preparing to enter college for the first time, while her five year-old son, Tristan, prepared to enter kindergarten, when the untimely news of her father's death had arrived. She was overwhelmed with sadness for weeks. It had been her desire to make her father proud by attending and graduating college. Especially since she knew how heartbroken he was after finding out that she'd become pregnant soon after graduating high school.

Her decision to go to college had brought an incredible joy to her father. Thrilled that she was finally going to get a college education, Everson Alexander had agreed to not only ante up the tuition costs, but also provide Paris and his grandson with monthly financial support until she graduated.

Tristan's father had no active role within his son's life and he provided Paris with no child support, financial or otherwise. When he'd learned that she was pregnant, his appearance in her life became less frequent. He'd only seen his son once and that was six months after she'd given birth.

His absence suited Paris just fine. She considered him to be trifling anyway and she wanted nothing to do with him.

Paris had been known to change jobs about as often as the weather forecast changed. But since learning of her father's wish that she and her sister run his ad agency, she'd become more determined than ever to try and fulfill his dream for them.

When Everson's Will had been drawn up he was quite aware of the skills that his daughters lacked, yet he had hoped that by the time the good Lord called him home, he would have not only persuaded both girls to join the agency, but that he would have also already taught them everything that they needed to know in order to survive and succeed within the advertising agency business.

A month prior to his death, he had reviewed the Will again with his attorney. It was at that time that he'd decided to add a provision in which he appointed Blade Barnes to serve as a special adviser to his daughters. However, full decision-making authority would remain squarely in the hands of Milan and Paris.

The twins' lack of experience and preparation to deal with such an enormous responsibility became too intriguing for the local and national media to ignore. Especially when it also became known that their father had raised them in a single parent household.

Milan's and Paris' mother abandoned them six months after she'd given birth. No reason was ever given for the sudden disappearance, aside from a note that their father had found one morning attached to the crib's wooden railing. His daughter's incessant crying had awakened him. It was as if they knew that something had gone terribly wrong.

The note simply said that their mother *needed to get away.* It had been the most difficult thing that Everson had ever read in his life. Later that day, he concluded that his wife, Nicole Alexander, must have gotten up in the wee hours of the morning. He often slept like a log so he would not have heard her when she got out of bed or her movements around the room. Although, she took none of her clothes, jewelry, credit cards or any other personal possessions. Even her Toyota 4Runner had remained parked in the garage.

Everson had tried assiduously to find his wife. He'd called her closest friends and sought any help that they might provide. But they knew no more than he did concerning her whereabouts. And her only family member was an estranged brother, Roberto Mendoza, who lived in Miami. Nicole had never known her father, and her mother had passed away a couple of years prior to her marriage to Everson.

He'd made several attempts to contact her brother on the telephone, and when he finally succeeded in reaching him, his wife's brother stated that he hadn't spoken to his sister in over six years. Then he politely requested that Everson not bother him again 'with all this nonsense'.

The assistance of the local authorities was also sought. They had come out and conducted a brief investigation of the matter before concluding that there was nothing they could do since there was no evidence of a crime having been committed, any signs of neither a break-in nor anything that would suggest foul play. Everson was not the least bit happy with their *assistance.* Of course there hadn't been any broken windows, or a trail of blood on the floor, but he tried to convince them that his wife had disappeared for no apparent reason. The officer in charge of the investigation had pulled him aside and explained that family abandonment happened more often than most people realized. And while most cases usually involved the husband walking away without a trace, women were known to do so as well. The officer's words provided little comfort to Everson.

Several days, weeks and months would eventually pass. Everson remained optimistic that his wife would return to her children – to him. He'd spent many agonizing days and nights trying to understand what would cause his wife – a mother – to just walk away from her family with no plausible explanation. He had tried to recall anything out of the ordinary that could have happened prior to her disappearance. An argument maybe. Perhaps something that he did or failed to do, which might have hurt her feelings or upset her in any way. But he could come up with nothing. Then he wondered if perhaps his wife had simply suffered a case of *postpartum depression*. Of course, he had no idea how long something like that could last.

After three arduous years had gone by, Everson's attempt to remain hopeful dissipated. Reluctantly, he drove to the courthouse in downtown Atlanta and filed a petition for divorce with the FULTON COUNTY SUPERIOR COURT, citing *desertion* as the grounds for the request.

The twins have no personal memories of their mother. After all, they were simply too young at the time. Everson had shown a handful of pictures of her to them. It was obvious that she was a beautiful woman. But even in those photographs, as beautiful as Nicole Alexander was, there had been a hint of unhappiness within her eyes. Her face seemed to be etched with sorrow. Her lips restricted, as if too stingy to smile.

Until they were age ten, Everson had led Milan and Paris to believe that their mother died during childbirth. But shortly after their tenth birthday, due in part to his unwillingness to allow such a lie to continue, Everson met with his daughters and shared the painful truth. Undoubtedly, it had been a conversation that he'd hoped would never occur.

Raising two infants alone was not an easy task for most, and especially not for a thirty-two year-old black male who was on track to become a partner at a leading management consulting firm. It was a rare career opportunity for him. One that didn't present itself often. Yet, Everson had made the tough decision to rearrange his priorities – his entire life. The twins became his number one focus. He resigned his position as an associate at the management consulting firm and immediately setup an office within his home where he began to work as an independent marketing consultant. This new avenue allowed him to avoid having to place the twins into a daycare facility, which he dreaded. And when the twins began school he found a certain satisfaction in being able to watch them board the school bus each morning and later stand and greet them when they arrived at the bus stop in the afternoon. He realized, however, that his dual roles over the years hadn't all been a piece of cake, by any means. But by the grace of God everything had turned out good.

Everson's sister lived nearby, which helped tremendously as the twins grew older. There were just some things that the girls were more comfortable discussing with another female, and he understood that quite well. Actually, he welcomed his sister's interest and involvement since she had no children of her own and had never married. Although his sister was the twins' Aunt Millie, she sort of took on the role of a surrogate mother to them, which meant a lot to Milan and Paris. To him as well.

CHAPTER
THREE

Milan and Paris were thirteen when their father had decided to start his own advertising agency. His job as an independent marketing consultant had netted him many contacts over the years, and he'd always had an interest in creating ads. He knew that all he needed was just one client to jumpstart the new venture.

It came one day in the form of a flyer that had been stuck on the outside of his mailbox. Such solicitations were not uncommon in their subdivision. Flyers and business cards peddling everything from house cleaning services to painting contractors found their way to his mailbox constantly. But, for some reason, this particular solicitation had caught his eye. It was from a landscaping business named EXSCAPES. Everson was intrigued by the name given the business and by the tagline on the flyer – EXSCAPE YOUR LANDSCAPE. The flyer mentioned that they specialized in complete residential and commercial landscaping services. Along with a business telephone number printed in large bold type, the name of the proprietor was also listed at the bottom of the flyer – RALEIGH ROBINSON.

After jotting down some ideas on paper, Everson had come up with a marketing campaign for EXSCAPES. Three phone calls later and he had an appointment to meet with Mr. Robinson to discuss his ideas. During their meeting, Everson soon discovered that EXSCAPES was only spending about forty thousand dollars a year on advertising. He convinced him to up it to seventy-five thousand and allow his firm, the ALEXANDER AGENCY, to handle all of his advertising and marketing needs. The skeptical Raleigh Robinson agreed, although not without some arm-twisting.

EXSCAPES became Everson's first client for his new ad agency. Soon thereafter other accounts, some quite prominent, came aboard as well. But Everson always tried to remember the one account that had gotten him started. And while EXSCAPES grew to eventually bill $3 million annually, it soon became a relatively small account among the agency's growing client roster. Yet, it was very important to Everson that EXSCAPES feel at home amongst his other clients, despite their much smaller ad budget.

It was on the night of *August 18, 2002* that everything abruptly changed. Fifty-seven year-old Everson Alexander became the fatal victim of a carjacking while driving home from his downtown office. His assailants were never identified and as a result, no arrests had been made.

Milan and Paris were devastated after learning of their father's tragedy. And since Everson was renowned throughout Atlanta's business and civic community, well-wishers poured in from all areas of Georgia. Professional colleagues and dignitaries alike had attended his funeral.

Once news broke that Milan and Paris had been appointed to assume leadership roles at the agency, their story quickly took on a life of its own.

The young women soon found themselves thrust into the media limelight. Interviews were conducted on every major morning news show. A front-page feature article appeared in the industry's leading periodical, ADVERTISING AGE. THE NEW YORK TIMES chronicled their story in one of its Sunday editions, and both ESSENCE and BLACK ENTERPRISE magazines published lengthy articles that praised the twins for their willingness to try and keep their father's legacy alive.

Blade Barnes, acting in his role as a special adviser, brought in some additional experts to try and give the twins a crash course on the advertising agency business. Behind closed doors others within the industry questioned Everson's decision to leave a multi-million dollar business solely in the hands of his young and inexperienced daughters. But Blade Barnes maintained a strong belief in the twins' ability to learn quickly. They would eventually prove him right. Within just a few months, Milan and Paris were showing some semblance of control at the agency. They both sat in on all client meetings as well as new business pitches. And while Milan involved herself more in the administrative functions of the agency, Paris became involved on the client services and creative sides.

It was Paris who'd made the tough decision to drop the agency's smaller, less lucrative accounts and place a greater emphasis on the larger, higher revenue producing accounts. After the house cleaning had taken place, a total of five accounts had been resigned by the agency, including EXSCAPES.

The ALEXANDER AGENCY also moved to new offices, relocating from downtown Atlanta to a new office building in the Perimeter Mall area in suburban Dunwoody. Neither sister wanted to fight a lot of traffic every morning since both lived just north of the Perimeter Mall. Although, with each of them now earning salaries, excluding bonuses, of $250,000 per year, new domiciles were certainly looming on the horizon.

Further making their mark on the ad agency, Milan and Paris realigned some of the staff, including the hiring of more women. Aunt Millie was also given a job within the agency's human resources department. It was the least they could do to show their appreciation to their aunt for helping to care for them over the years.

One year later, it was clear that Milan and Paris Alexander were in charge. The skeptics and nay Sayers had all been silenced, at least for now. With an accomplished staff supporting their efforts, the ALEXANDER AGENCY appeared to be sailing smoothly. Aside from the accounts that they chose to resign, no other clients had jumped ship. In fact, the agency was currently in the middle of an ad review to try and win the SOME BODY FITNESS CENTERS account, which could possibly garner them an additional $20 million annually.

The mood at the agency, however, was quite somber on this Tuesday afternoon. The reason being, it was the first anniversary of Everson's death. Colleagues and friends had sent over an abundance of flowers and heartfelt cards. Others made brief phone calls offering words of encouragement. Everson Alexander had been respected by many and loved by all who knew him.

Just before the Tuesday workday began, Milan and Paris had instructed all of the employees to pause for five minutes in a moment of silence and prayer. Everyone had willingly participated, regardless of his or her religious beliefs.

The two of them, along with Aunt Millie, had convened in Milan's office where they kneeled on the floor beside her desk, held hands and prayed. When the prayer had ended, the trio engaged one another in comforting hugs. Then they cried.

No one knew precisely when his time on this earth would end. It was just another intricacy of life that has confounded man since the beginning of time. Most people dealt with it by simply choosing not to think about it at all. But everything had its proper time. Indeed, a time to be born and a time to die. Focusing on that undeniable fact forced a person to look at life with some sense of perspective. Everson Alexander had viewed life in such a manner. He chose not to spend his time on that which made no real difference. He was not a perfect man by anyone's definition of perfection. Yet, he never failed in his care and concern for the well being of others. And when he became a wealthy man, he understood clearly that he then had a responsibility to use his wealth – his blessings – to effectively serve others.

It was a belief by some that people's lives could be changed somewhat by the death of another. Everson's death had certainly affected change in many.

Perhaps the only way for the living to truly understand and appreciate life was by attending a funeral. Only then could the everyday hustle and bustle around them take a respite. Funerals tended to have an uncanny way of making people put their life in its truest perspective. They caused you to focus on those who were most important; allowed you to release unresolved anger or conflict. The only problem, however, was that for most, once the grieving period ended, perhaps just a couple of days later, the concerns of life had a peculiar way of once again becoming center stage.

CHAPTER
FOUR

Raleigh Robinson parked the Buick into a slot that was only a few feet from the front doors of the upscale office building. He had to circle the parking lot several times before he spotted a woman vacating the space. He thought that he might have to fight for the coveted parking space when another driver attempted to pull into the spot ahead of him. Raleigh honked his horn once and then stared the driver down. The driver acquiesced and then drove away. This simply wasn't a good day for anyone to push his buttons.

He shut off the car's engine, listening as it coughed and rattled for a few seconds before finally becoming silent. He wasn't quite sure why he was hanging onto this old rusting piece of crap. He could have purchased a brand new Park Avenue many times over the years. Instead, he chose to cart himself around in one that was obviously on its last leg – or tire.

As far as appearances go, Raleigh Robinson certainly did not look like the owner of a million-dollar landscaping business. He didn't wear expensive clothes, fine jewelry or splurge on any of the usual luxuries that anyone else in his position might have taken advantage of. Raleigh was about as frugal as they come.

He peered through the car's windshield, gazing up at the windows that framed the eighth floor of the twelve-story office building. The rays from the sun danced off the reflective glass like ballerinas, making it impossible to see through them. But he quickly realized that from his vantage point he couldn't see up there anyway – his vision was never twenty-twenty. Yet, he knew they were both up there. Probably acting like they owned the world. He doubted that they even remembered that today was the anniversary of their father's death. He gritted his teeth. They were too busy spending their time decorating and behaving like they were running some sort of sorority house.

"Don't party yourselves out little girls," he whispered, his voice full of spite. "Because I'm about to *really* get this party started!"

Raleigh took in a few deep breaths. His hands were beginning to shake a little. Trying to calm himself, he rubbed his hands against the legs of his jeans. He was sweating like a hog in a sauna. He continued to sit in the car for a few more minutes. With his hands balled into a tight fist, he closed his eyes and repeatedly told himself to *get a grip.*

This is the day that he'd been anxiously waiting for. It had been almost five months since he received the *letter* from them. At first he thought that perhaps there had been some kind of a mistake. Perhaps a clerical error. Surely they were not dropping him from their client roster? After all, it was *his business* that had gotten *their business* off the ground. Where was the loyalty? The appreciation? The quid pro quo?

"They were too young and naïve to understand anything about loyalty and appreciation," he muttered acidly.

Raleigh began to feel nauseating spurts of adrenaline course through his veins. Then the veins in his neck began to stand out in livid ridges. The spasm of irritation crossing his chunky face was palpable. He looked down at his hands. They were wet again. He couldn't believe how much he was sweating. Perspiration slid steadily from his armpits like rain sliding down a windowpane. His stomach was in knots, and his heart was turning flip-flops inside his chest like a skilled gymnast.

The time had arrived, however. He was convinced that he'd reached the point of no return. Getting cold feet was no longer an option. His desire to set matters straight was like a raging fire burning inside his belly.

A resounding voice began to echo within his ears. *Quench the fire, Raleigh! Quench the fire!* He shook his head violently, hoping to silence the echoes, but they seemed to only get louder. Unable to endure it any longer, he thrust open the car door and tore from the vehicle. He staggered on the pavement momentarily as he lost his sense of equilibrium. Once composed, Raleigh slammed the door to the driver's side. Then he trotted around the car to the passenger's door and reached inside to grab the attaché case. He stood beside the car for a few seconds to slow his breathing and to glance around to see if there were any onlookers. Only the distant sound of cars passing on nearby I-285 and the chirping of birds could be heard.

Convinced that all was in order, he made his way towards the office building, purposely walking proudly, with a stately carriage about him. The attaché case was tucked beneath his arm.

There was only one way that this inevitable saga would end. He was determined to see to that.

CHAPTER
FIVE

Stepping from the plush elevators onto the eighth floor at the PERIMETER PROMENADE office building was like walking into a top New York modeling agency. From the incredibly gorgeous receptionist and various assistants, to those bearing management titles, beautifully attired women dotted the ALEXANDER AGENCY'S eighth floor haven like a fashion spread in VOGUE magazine. Some seventy-percent of the advertising agency's eighty-seven employees were female. The majority of workers were under the age of forty. And ever since the twins took control of the agency a year ago it quickly became a resume magnet.

Hiring solicitations continued to pour in on a weekly basis, mostly from men between the ages of twenty-one and sixty. Some even offering to take huge pay cuts just for an opportunity to work for the $125 million in annual billings agency. It had once been rumored that a high-ranking official in the governor's office was willing to resign in exchange for a senior management role at the agency. The rumor, however, was neither confirmed nor denied by the governor's staff.

With his eyes smoldering as they began raking the opulent surroundings once he'd exited from the elevator, Raleigh Robinson edged cautiously towards the receptionist's desk. As he moved along, his eyes continued to probe every square inch of the *new* ALEXANDER AGENCY. He was certain that Everson never would have allowed all this. The place was littered with a bunch of flowers everywhere, and the walls were all painted in female colors. The place resembled nothing like the downtown office that he had often visited.

Still clutching the black attaché case beneath his arm, Raleigh was nearly run over by one of the agency's staffers as she bolted from a nearby office and sprinted towards the elevators. "I'm so sorry sir!" she hastily apologized, though she never once made eye contact with him. Raleigh's teeth clamped as he shot her an annoying glance while watching her disappear into the elevator.

Conspicuously clad in a red football jersey, some nearly worn-out jeans and a pair of rundown white sneakers, Raleigh fixed his gaze onto the receptionist. He figured that she couldn't have been more than seventeen, although she was actually twenty-one. He found her to be quite pretty, but he was a bit dismayed by the low-cut blouse that she was wearing. Everson never would have hired her with that floozy look.

When he finally reached the receptionist's desk, which was shaped into a semi-circle, the young woman immediately held up one finger, signaling for him to wait a moment while she transferred a couple of calls. Afterwards, she greeted him with a warm and polite smile. "Good afternoon, sir. How can I help you?"

Raleigh attempted to slow his breathing once again before answering. "Uh, I . . . I need to see Paris Alexander." It had been Paris' name that was signed on the letter, so she would be priority number one.

The receptionist eyed him guardedly while unashamedly scrutinizing his very appearance. Probably considered him to be some bum off the streets, Raleigh thought to himself.

"Sir, do you have an appointment with Miss Alexander?" she asked.

Raleigh nodded. "No, I do not," he answered in a firm voice. "I'm a client."

"Of ours?" she uttered, failing miserably to hide her skepticism.

For a moment he considered taking her *out* right then and there. Who did she think she was? He simply couldn't understand why some black people always tried to give other black people a hard time – give them just a little bit of authority and their cocky heads swelled like a balloon filling with air. Hadn't we all endured the same struggles?

"What difference does it make, young lady," he answered tersely. "I expect to be treated with some dignity and respect whether I'm a client of this ad agency or from some other one, in which case I'd then be a *potential client*, wouldn't you agree?"

She feigned a smile. "I'm not trying to be disrespectful, sir. It's just that neither Milan nor Paris will see anyone without an appointment," she attempted to explain away her arrogance.

Raleigh simply glared at her as his blood began to boil.

She continued, "You have to understand that we're a very busy agency."

Raising his voice, Raleigh replied, "And I don't have all day to stand here twiddling my thumbs either!" He then leaned his massive frame over her desk. "Now, I suggest that you take your pretty little fingers and punch in whatever numbers will ring Paris' office and tell her that *Mister Raleigh Robinson* from EXSCAPES is here to see her. And I suggest that you make it clear to her that I'm not leaving until I have done so!"

"Sir, I think you better leave before I have to call security," she threatened.

Raleigh's boiling point had been reached. His patience evaporated as quickly as a cube of ice on a scorching sidewalk. He plopped the attaché case down onto her desk. "I guess we're going to have to do this the hard way," he told her through gritted teeth.

Speechless, the receptionist watched nervously as Raleigh used his thumbs to quickly pop open the attaché case. He then reached inside and pulled out a shiny revolver, shoving it into her face. She recoiled in horror. "Get up!" he ordered. "You and I are going to take a little walk through the premises." He concealed the weapon beneath his jersey inside the front part of his pants. Grabbing her forcefully by the arm, Raleigh led the young woman away from her desk. She was seized with fear. "Take me to Paris' office!" he demanded. "And don't even think about screaming or getting any other *funny* ideas or the last thing you hear will be the sound of a bullet ripping through your pretty little skull."

With her face suddenly a mask of terror, the receptionist began to lead the way to Paris' office. He warned her not to make eye contact with anyone as they moved down the corridor.

Unfortunately, no one had seen or heard the commotion up front since the receptionist area was somewhat isolated. Ordinarily, people were in and out of the elevators, which were directly in front of the receptionist station, but since it was the lunch hour, most of the employees had already departed the premises for their favorite restaurant or simply to bask in the glow of the day's sunshine.

The receptionist did as Raleigh had told her. Staring straight ahead, she weaved her way around cubicles and down another corridor that would dead-end into both Milan's and Paris' office. A couple of co-workers spoke to her as she passed them but she didn't return their greetings. The lunatic was nearly glued to her side. His beefy fingers were squeezing her arm while his other fat hand was positioned closely to the handle of the revolver, ready to yank it out should she be stupid enough to try and create a disturbance.

When they reached the end of the corridor they were standing in front of two large doors that were adjacent to one another. Both were closed. Raleigh glanced at the brass nameplates affixed to the mahogany wood doors. Their offices just had to be side by side, he thought to himself. Typical twins. Always having to dress alike, talk alike and trying to do everything else alike. Wasn't it enough that they looked alike?

Well, today he would continue their little trend by making certain that they also be *destroyed* alike.

CHAPTER
SIX

The receptionist stared at Raleigh as she nervously awaited his next instruction. He jerked his head to the right towards Paris' door, indicating that he wanted her to knock on it.

Reluctantly, she coiled her shaking hand into a fist and rapped her knuckles against the door in three successive knocks.

"You may come in," came the voice from the other side of the door, unaware of the impending danger.

The receptionist hesitated as she took hold of the door handle. Part of her wanted to scream some kind of warning to Paris, but she thought better of it. He pressed his fingernails into her skin. "Open it!" he told her, attempting to keep his voice low. She turned the handle and pushed the door forward.

When the two of them had entered the office, Paris was seated in a pink leather chair behind her platinum-framed desk. Her head appeared to be buried into a file. It wasn't until she heard the door close behind her *visitors* that she looked up. "Hey, Belinda," she spoke to the receptionist. She wasn't familiar with the gentleman accompanying her. After the twins had assumed control of the ad agency, one of the first things on their agenda was to schedule introductory meetings with the point-of-contacts on all of their accounts. However, since EXSCAPES was one of the clients that was to be resigned, no meeting was ever scheduled with Raleigh Robinson. Thus,

Paris had no idea who the strange-looking, overweight man was. She assumed that maybe it was Belinda's father and they'd stopped by for her to meet him. But the man had absolutely no resemblance to Belinda.

"What's up, guys?" she greeted them, rising from her chair.

Raleigh found himself momentarily mesmerized by Paris Alexander. He had never actually met Everson's daughters. He'd seen them from a distance at the funeral. And while he had seen their images splashed throughout the media over the past several months, seeing Paris in person for the first time seem to have caught him by surprise. She was a blushing beauty of chocolate curls that cascaded well beyond the slender shoulders of her petite body.

Belinda remained terrified and speechless. Trepidation covered her face like a deer caught in headlights.

Paris detected that something wasn't right. "Belinda?" she spoke, making her way towards the two of them. But before she reached them, Raleigh, snapping back to reality, shoved the receptionist directly into Paris, knocking her off balance. Instinctively, Paris grabbed Belinda by the waist to keep herself from falling backwards. "What the . . ." she began, but her sentence was cut short as she watched the large black man pull a gun from beneath his jersey.

Raleigh raised the gun to his shoulder level and aimed it at the two women. "Don't say another word!" he yelled.

Paris realized that she couldn't have said anything if she wanted to, because at the moment all words seemed have escaped her like a prisoner on the run. Her eyes widened with alarm as she backed into her desk. Belinda was clinging to her like a toddler unwilling to be left alone with the babysitter

Holding the gun steady with his right hand, Raleigh used the back of his left hand to wipe perspiration from his forehead. He could feel his mouth going dry as he watched them standing in rigid terror. "Do you know who I am?" he asked, his eyes fixed on Paris.

She studied his face carefully, trying desperately to recall anything about him or a particular gathering where they may have met. There were no recollections of any kind popping into her head. She had no idea who this man was, and for a moment she wondered if that was a *good* or a *bad* thing.

Raleigh concluded that her silence had answered his question. He knew that she had no clue who he was. He shifted his gaze to Belinda. "Tell her who I am!" he bellowed.

Belinda's entire body began to tremble, as if she'd just come in from the freezing cold with no clothes on. Paris pulled her closer so that they now embraced one another. She stared into the frightened woman's eyes in an attempt to assure her that everything would be all right.

Raleigh became agitated that she hadn't done what he'd just told her. "Did you not hear me, woman!" his voice exploded. "I said to tell her who I am!"

A strangled cry erupted from Belinda's lips. "I don't know who you are!" she cried, her voice high and hysterical.

"And why is that?" Raleigh shouted, moving a step closer to them. "Could it be because I didn't spend enough money with your little agency? Could it be because you all never took the time to introduce yourselves to me? Or, could it simply be because none of you give a rat's behind who I am!"

His ranting made Paris realize that he could possibly be a disgruntled client or a former employee. "Sir, please just tell us who you are, okay? Tell us what it is that you want from us?" she pleaded.

Raleigh's eyes narrowed in disgust. "So you think this black man wants or needs something from you!" He stalked over to them and pushed them away from the desk. "Sit your butts over there!" he ordered, pointing to the pink leather sofa positioned in a corner of Paris' spacious office.

They stumbled towards the sofa and sat, arms clinging to one another like the Olympic rings logo.

Raleigh glared at Paris. "I can see that you're nothing but an over privileged, arrogant and spoiled little brat!"

Paris bristled at his harsh and demeaning words.

"News flash for you, Miss Alexander!" he began. "I am the *first* client that your daddy signed when he started this ad agency!"

The revelation surprised Paris. She quickly began to put the pieces together in her head. He had to be one of the clients that they had resigned a few months ago.

Raleigh continued. "But you wouldn't know that, would you, Miss Alexander? I mean, after all, you were just a kid at "the time, huh? Running around playing with your cute Barbie dolls!"

"Which client are you?" Paris asked helplessly. "What's the name of your company?"

Raleigh laughed insipidly. "Unbelievable!" he cackled. Then, like a mad man, he shoved his hand into the back pocket of his jeans and fished out a crumpled piece of paper. "Allow me to refresh your memory!" he told Paris as he unfurled the paper and then dangled it in front of her face, holding it just close enough for her to see the letterhead's insignia bearing the name of the ALEXANDER AGENCY.

Paris recognized the letter immediately. It was one of five that she'd sent to the clients they were no longer interested in retaining on their roster. She felt sick to her stomach. She had no idea that she had gotten rid of the very first client that her father had began the agency with. She tried to imagine how this man must have been feeling. He'd obviously gone off the deep end. Thoughts of Tristan surfaced in her mind. Her son needed his mother. She couldn't allow anything to happen to her. She prayed silently that God would not allow this idiot to harm her.

Taking a deep breath, Paris began, "Um . . . so, you're Mr. Robinson?"

He snatched the letter from her view and stuffed it back into his pocket. "What do you think?" he answered sarcastically.

She glanced at Belinda, whose already fair-skinned complexion appeared devoid of any color whatsoever. She decided to try and appease the man. "Mr. Robinson, I'm sure we can straighten this whole thing out," she told him.

Raleigh snickered liked a schoolboy who'd just gotten away with pulling a wild prank. "Yeah, right! I suppose you're going to tell me that everything was some big mistake? That you didn't intend to drop the one client that gave this agency its start? That instead of me receiving some *Dear John* letter, that I should have received a polite phone call scheduling a meeting with me, huh? Is that what you mean by 'straighten out'?"

Before Paris could answer, Belinda spoke. "What she's trying to say is . . ."

Her words were interrupted when Raleigh reached over and grabbed her by the arm, yanking her from the sofa. Belinda emitted a faint scream as her body stiffened in apprehension. He pressed the gun to the side of her forehead. Paris covered her mouth in horror. "I've had just about enough of your sassy mouth, little Missy! When I want your opinion I'll ask for it!" he barked the words into her ear. "Do you understand me?"

Belinda's head began to move up and down like a bobble head doll.

Raleigh then shoved the young woman towards the sofa again, but with so much force that Belinda's tiny body missed the sofa entirely. She crashed into a glass end table that was next to the sofa. The collision sent her buckling at the knees, which then caused her to hit her head on the edge of the table. Like a rag doll, her body crumpled to the floor.

"Oh my god!" Paris shouted, bolting from the sofa. She attempted to make a beeline to Belinda, but the sudden pop and then the sound of glass shattering stopped her cold. Raleigh had fired a bullet through the window.

"Back on the sofa!" he said sharply.

Paris slowly resumed her position.

"Consider that a *warning* shot," he told her as he aimed the gun in her direction. "It won't be *glass* shattering the next time."

Paris felt as if a heavy fist was closing over her heart. She could see a trail of blood making its descent down Belinda's face. She prayed that she'd only been knocked unconscious. Although it was frightening to see the lifeless body of one of their employees sprawled across the floor right in front of her eyes. And there was nothing she could do about it. She was hoping that someone had heard the gunshot. Then it dawned on her that Milan was right next door. *God, please don't let my sister come in here.*

Paris wiped away tears with her index finger. Her eyes turned to Raleigh. He returned a fixed level stare on her. The venom consuming his dark eyes was clear and present. She was trying desperately to maintain her composure, but quickly found herself being seized by a band of tears. Her gentle eyes were unable to restrain their attack. And like a defeated athlete, Paris dropped her head, surrendering to a flood of emotions.

Raleigh Robinson smiled nastily, staring at her as if she was a cockroach that needed to be stepped on. "This is going to be more fun than I ever imagined," he murmured.

CHAPTER SEVEN

Milan Alexander had been speaking on the telephone with a client when she heard what sounded like a firecracker and then glass breaking. She quickly brought the call to an end and then dialed her sister's extension. The phone rang several times without an answer. She hung up and bolted from her desk. As she arrived in the hallway she was met by one of the agency's account managers.

"Did you hear that noise?" Milan asked her, as the two of them stood in front of the door to Paris' office. The account manager's office was located on the other side of Paris'.

"Yeah, I heard it. I think it came from your sister's office."

Milan began knocking on Paris' door. "Paris, are you in there?" She waited a few seconds, but after getting no response she grabbed the door handle and thrust open the door. The account manager was right on her heels.

Both her mind and heart began to race frantically when she saw Belinda sprawled across the floor, and a small pool of blood accumulating on the carpet beneath her face. "Call nine-one-one!" Milan shouted as she darted towards the lifeless body of Belinda. But before either of them could even consider what to do next, the door slammed shut behind them.

Startled, they both turned around immediately. Their mouths dropped and their eyes bulged simultaneously as they came face to face with the heavy-set black man with a wild

Afro. He had one arm wrapped around Paris' neck with his hand covering her mouth, and his other hand holding a gun that was pointed precisely in their direction.

"Don't move!" Raleigh yelled.

Milan's heart was pounding so fast that she thought she was going to pass out.

Raleigh motioned with the weapon for Milan and the account manager to move over towards the door.

They complied.

He took quick notice of the other sister. He found it surprising that they didn't have the *same* hairstyle. While her sister sported an abundance of long black curls, Milan's black mane was worn long and straight. He couldn't help but notice how shiny her hair was, glistening like a diamond in a jeweler's display case.

Refusing to allow himself to be sidetracked by their awesome beauty, he shoved Paris toward the other two. Paris threw her arms around her sister, nearly hysterical with tears. Milan held onto her with all of her being. "What's going on?" she whispered in her sister's ear. Paris attempted to explain the situation but Raleigh quickly ordered her to shut up!

"Let's go!" he barked, motioning the three of them out of the office.

Paris glanced over at Belinda's body. "Please!" she begged. "Let me help her. She could be dying!"

Raleigh turned a cold eye towards Belinda. "She won't be going anywhere anytime soon," he remarked. He then instructed the women to move to the receptionist area, cautioning them along the way not to try and get *cute*.

The offices were nearly empty since it was still the lunchtime hour. When they arrived at the receptionist's station, Raleigh ordered Paris to get on the intercom and have anyone who was still in the office to come up front immediately.

"What should I tell them?" she asked him.

"Aren't you their boss?" he answered. "I don't care what you have to tell them, just get them all out here!"

With obvious reluctance in her eyes and her body language, Paris lifted the switchboard's receiver. "Attention all employees," she began. With her voice cracking at times, she went on to make the *very important* announcement. Afterwards, following Raleigh's orders, she shut down the switchboard so that all incoming calls went directly into the employees' voice mailboxes.

Minutes later, several employees had made their way from various cubicles, which littered the eighth floor like tepees on a reservation. Others had come from private offices, while a few had to abandon tuna and turkey sandwiches as they scurried from the break room.

Before long, the lobby of the ALEXANDER AGENCY had filled with some twenty-three employees, including Milan and Paris. For whatever reasons, this group had chosen not to leave the office for lunch on this particular day. It was a decision that most would later regret. Aunt Millie had been one of the majority who'd chosen to have lunch away from the office.

Only five of the twenty-three were men.

Unaware of why they'd been summoned for the impromptu meeting, the air quickly filled with chatter. The twins attempted to quiet the bunch as they sensed that their captor seemed to be getting annoyed.

Raleigh had positioned himself behind Belinda's desk. For the moment, the gun was shielded once again inside the front of jeans. He whipped it out and held the weapon above his head, pointed at the ceiling. "QUIET!" he shouted. All whispering and chattering came to an abrupt end. There were a few gasps from some of the women when their eyes locked onto the gun.

"This is a hostage situation!" his voice thundered. "And I am the one who's in control!"

Several employees began to clutch one another. A couple of the men took a step in Raleigh's direction. He quickly pointed the gun squarely on the two would-be heroes. "I wouldn't get any smart ideas right now if I were you," he warned them.

"Everyone, please do as he says," Paris intervened.

The men retreated, deciding that it was best to accept their roles as living cowards rather than dead heroes.

Raleigh ordered them all to move to the other side of the receptionist area and stand against the wall.

"What does he want?" Milan whispered to her sister, as they led the employees across the room.

Paris peeked over at Raleigh, who, at the moment, seemed to be pondering his next move. "He was daddy's first client when the agency was started," she whispered back.

"Which client?"

"The landscaping account."

"EXSCAPES?"

Paris nodded. "He was one of the five accounts that we resigned."

"Oh my god," Milan mumbled. "Is he angry at us for dropping him?"

Paris couldn't believe that her sister was asking such a dumb question. "Milan, the man has taken us hostage, okay?"

Before Milan could respond, Raleigh fired another bullet through a wall of windows that consumed one side of the room. More glass shattered. Pieces landed inside on the floor as well as outside on the pavement below. "Enough with the talking!" he shouted, clearly annoyed and seemingly unsure of his next move. He could hear his own heavy breathing within his ears. A tiny cell phone was pulled from his front pocket. He demanded to know the phone number for the building's security downstairs.

Paris unwillingly became the group's spokesperson. She gave him the number for the security office. She surprised herself by the fact that she knew the telephone number by heart. But then she remembered calling them just last night after working late to have someone escort her to her car.

All eyes were focused on Raleigh Robinson as his massive fingers began pouncing on the small keypad. When the security office answered the call, he cleared his throat excessively and then began to speak. "Whom am I speaking to?"

"This is Mike at the security desk."

"Well, listen up Mikey. I have taken control of the offices on the eighth floor. There are many hostages. You may have heard some shots being fired. They were from the gun that I have in my possession. There will undoubtedly be more shots before all is said and done . . ."

"Who is this?" the security officer interrupted.

"My identity isn't important right now, Mikey."

"Is this some kind of a prank call?"

Raleigh became irritated. "You're not a very good listener, Mikey. The last person who didn't listen to me is now lying on the floor in the other room in a nice puddle of blood."

"Okay, okay. I hear ya," Mike replied. "Don't freak out on me."

Hearts were pounding loudly and collectively from the employees as they continued to listen to their captor talk with such ease about their situation.

"First, you need to shut off the elevator that leads to this floor. No one should attempt to come up here unless I say so," Raleigh began laying down his instructions. "If anyone steps from that elevator onto this floor, I will not hesitate to put a bullet through their head, understood?"

Mike answered in the affirmative as he was quickly jotting down notes on a legal pad.

"I also want a news crew at the building within the next twenty minutes," Raleigh continued. "However, I only want CHANNEL TWO news people. One cameraman and one reporter."

Mike attempted to explain that he didn't think that he could handle Raleigh's request within such a short period of time.

"You can and you will," Raleigh politely told him. "And the reporter must be *Monica Kaufman*. No one else will suffice."

Mike wanted to know how to reach him. Raleigh rattled off his cell phone number without hesitation, like he was placing a fast food order at the drive-through. "Call me when Monica Kaufman has arrived," he said before terminating the call.

Raleigh moved from behind the desk and walked over to his captives. He looked them over, his eyes roving maniacally. "Why are there more women than men at this agency?" he demanded to know.

Seized with fear, no one dared to answer him. The eerie silence hung suspended in the air like the noonday clouds. Within the past few minutes, each of them had recalled to mind the office shootings that had taken place in the Buckhead area of Atlanta some five years ago – July 1999 – when a disgruntled *day trader* took the lives of nine people and wounded thirteen others within the offices of a brokerage firm before later killing himself. Hours earlier, the infamous *Mark Barton* had killed his entire family while they slept. Friends and acquaintances would later describe the killer as friendly and normal.

The impending massacre that Raleigh Robinson had in mind would undoubtedly be far worse. The headlines perhaps even bigger. Would anyone later describe this former client as *friendly* and *normal*?

"Miss Alexander, I asked you a question? Surely you do not refuse to answer me?"

Although there were two *Miss Alexanders*, Paris assumed that he was speaking to her since his dark cold eyes appeared to be fixed on her. "Uh . . . Um, most of our employees are out to lunch," she stated nervously.

"Is that so? Are you telling me that if *everyone* were here, right now, there'd be more *men* than women?"

Paris dropped her head and stared at the floor.

"Just what I thought," Raleigh said, laughing to himself. He looked over towards the five men, who had all huddled, as if they were secretly plotting against him. "Tell you what guys, when I'm finished here, I'll make certain that there's an *even* representation at this agency." He used the gun as a pointer and began to count heads. "Mmm, eighteen women and only five men. That's not fair, now is it?" He cocked the gun and aimed it at one of the women. She froze in utter fear.

"Mr. Robinson, please don't?" Paris begged him. Milan echoed the same.

Raleigh ignored them both. Increasing his grip around the revolver he closed one eye and squinted the other one as if he was zeroing in on a precise target on the woman's body. The middle-aged woman remained frozen. Images of her husband and three children flashed rapidly across her mind like flashes from a camera in the hands of a skilled photographer. She didn't want to die. Not like this. Not by him.

Another woman who was standing next to the *targeted* woman, held onto one of her hands tightly. She refused to let go, even as the terrified middle-aged woman's body began to shake uncontrollably.

"BANG!" Raleigh shouted in a loud booming voice, scaring the living daylights out of everyone. He then lowered the gun and roared with laughter. The middle-aged woman buried her head into the arms of the other woman and sobbed hysterically.

Still laughing, Raleigh wiped his face with the back of his hand. "That was a good one! You all should have seen the look on your faces! Now, you can't buy that kind of creativity!" He threw his big noggin back and laughed some more, his fat round belly bouncing up and down wildly beneath his jersey.

CHAPTER
EIGHT

Sirens were soon heard from outside the window. Raleigh crept over and peered below. White and blue Fulton County police cars dotted the parking lot. There were a couple of fire engines and at least three ambulances. Raleigh couldn't quite figure out why there were fire trucks. He hadn't planned on setting the building on fire. And he was reasonably certain that those ladders couldn't reach the eighth floor. Perhaps they were just preparing for the worst. And they were smart to be doing so.

The sudden swoop of a CHANNEL TWO news helicopter flying past the window nearly startled him. They had brought *Monica!* Just as he requested.

Raleigh had always admired the popular local anchorwoman. He had hoped to one day be featured on one of her TV specials – MONICA KAUFMAN CLOSE UP – to discuss the success of his landscaping business. He'd even practiced his interview many times in the living room of his home, which was where he'd been planning to have her conduct the interview. And already set aside in his closet was a dark blue suit that he was going to wear for the special occasion.

He glanced at his current wardrobe. Why hadn't he thought to wear the suit today? He felt somewhat ashamed that Monica would have to see him this way. And his *Don King* hairstyle wasn't helping his appearance much either. He cursed himself for not getting a haircut. He hoped that Monica would look past his outward appearance. He was also hoping that she'd forgive him for having to conduct the interview under slightly different circumstances.

Raleigh moved away from the window and positioned himself behind the receptionist's desk again. The switchboard rang loudly, causing him to jump. "I thought I told you to shut this thing down!" he screamed across the room towards Paris.

Paris didn't respond. Immense fear had already taken control of her body and it seemed to be growing like cancer.

Unwilling to listen to the annoying rings any longer, Raleigh took a step back from the desk and then pointed the revolver at the console and pumped two bullets into the center of it. The employees all let out a collective gasp as the shots were fired. Sparks and white smoke erupted from the machine immediately. But he had accomplished his task – the ringing ceased.

He moved away from the desk once again and stood in front of his captives, being sure to keep a watchful eye on the elevators. The whirling sound of several helicopters from outside the building could now be heard. He was fairly certain that S.W.A.T. officers were also being strategically placed on rooftops and on other floors. The trigger-happy combative men probably couldn't wait to have a shot at him. A chance to take out another black man. But Raleigh was quite confident that there would be no need for the *special weapons and tactics* team. Not here. Not today.

His breathing grew heavy again. He took some deep breaths, wiping perspiration from his face and then drying his hand on his jersey. "What day is it, Miss Alexander?" the question came from out of the blue.

"Excuse me?" Paris replied, her voice cracking still.

"I said what *day* is it! Have you suddenly become deaf?"

Averting her gaze from his, Paris answered, "Today is Tuesday, Mr. Robinson."

Raleigh snickered menacingly. "Oh, how soon we forget! The both of you ought to be ashamed of yourselves! You're both where you are today because of your father – whose death occurred one year ago today! Have you no sense of memorial for the man?"

Milan and Paris exchanged bewildering glances. "We are aware of that, Mr. Robinson," Milan spoke. "That's the reason for all the flowers that you see around the office," she explained, pointing to the assortment of beautiful flowers that were scattered throughout the receptionist's area.

Raleigh allowed his eyes to survey the room, his gaze picking out vases containing various flower arrangements. For a moment, grief and sadness began to overcome him. His chin sunk dejectedly into his chest. He gave a deep sigh and told himself to *get a grip*. It was the ringing of his cell phone that caused him to focus once again on the situation at hand.

While Raleigh answered the call, Paris took the opportunity to speak to her sister. "Listen, Milan. The man is obviously crazy. I think we should consider rushing him all at once. I mean there's twenty-three of us and only one of him," she reasoned.

"Yes, but he's the *one* with the gun, Paris. I say we just remain calm and wait for the police to do their job."

"Wait nothing! Milan, the man is planning to kill every last one of us. You heard what he said on the phone. Now, I assume that he's only got two bullets left and . . ."

"How do you know how many bullets he has left? Milan interrupted.

"Because he fired one through the window in my office, he fired another one through the window out here, and he just fired two into the darn switchboard. That's *four* bullets. The gun probably only holds six."

"Well, we don't know that for sure, Paris. Besides, what's to stop him for reloading the gun with more bullets from his pocket or something?"

"First of all, we'd be stupid to just stand here and watch him reload his gun. And second of all, you don't see him carrying any other bullets. I mean, the only thing bulging from his pockets is that cell phone."

Milan shook her head. "I don't know, Paris."

"Milan, if he's going to take us out, which is exactly what he's planning to do, then I say we at least go out with a fight, and not like some helpless punks. I mean you have no idea how scared I am right now of losing my life – losing my son."

Tears streamed down Paris' face. Milan squeezed her

sister's hand. "Paris, it's all right to be scared. But it's not all right to be stupid!"

Hearing Raleigh's voice raise an octave quickly ended their discussion. "Don't try and play me for a fool!" he shouted into the cell phone. "Get me Monica Kaufman or I start dropping bodies!" He ended the call and shoved the phone back into the front pocket of his jeans. He'd clearly become upset by the phone conversation.

"That's it! I've had enough!" he yelled. He grabbed the person who happened to be closest to him and shoved her towards the elevators. The victim was a young woman from the media department. She'd just been married a month ago. Tears flooded the young woman's face causing black mascara to run wildly down her puffy cheeks.

"Please, sir . . ." she begged.

"Too late!" Raleigh snapped. He pointed the gun squarely between her eyes. Instinctively, she covered her face with both hands. Her petite frame quickly sunk to the floor. The others could only watch in horror as one of their own was about to be taken out by this idiot.

Raleigh's hand began to shake. He tried to steady the gun. His breathing grew more intense. Perspiration consumed his face and neck like a torrential rain. Then his big ol' body began to wobble and his vision started to blur.

"Quench the fire, Raleigh! Quench the fire!" He began to hear those words over and over in his head.

For a split second, one of the men considered tackling him with all the force and determination inside an Atlanta Falcons' right tackle, who sought revenge on the opposing team's quarterback – even though Raleigh was probably at least twice his size.

Then it became obvious that he wouldn't have to rush the big man after all. Everything seemed to happen in slow motion. The silver gun dropped from Raleigh's hand and hit the deep pile carpeted floor with a thud. He then brought both hands to his chest. His massive fingers were strangling a handful of his red jersey as he clutched it tightly. His eyes appeared to roll around. His eyelids blinked several times before closing altogether, as his huge body began to convulse before finally falling forward.

One of the men raced over and retrieved the gun from the floor. Another one rushed to comfort the young woman crouched by the elevator, who moments ago thought that her life was about to come to a violent end. Paris sprinted down the corridor to her office, praying all the way that Belinda was still alive. Milan quickly disappeared into a nearby cubicle and got on the phone and dialed the number to the security desk downstairs. Everyone else breathed a sigh of relief as they gathered around the body of their captor. Another gentleman kneeled next to Raleigh's body and checked his pulse. He would check it several times before rising from the floor and quietly announcing that Raleigh Robinson was dead.

CHAPTER NINE

Three months had passed since the hostage ordeal by Raleigh Robinson. Things appeared to be business as usual at the ALEXANDER AGENCY. Of course security had been increased around the office building, and no visitors were allowed to board the elevators to any floor within the building without an escort from the company that they were visiting. This new procedure suited all the employees on the eighth floor just fine.

Belinda's unexpected meeting with the glass end table had only knocked her unconscious, but it did leave her with a concussion as well as a nasty scar. The receptionist was just thankful to be alive.

It was later learned that Raleigh's landscaping business had actually begun to collapse a couple of months prior to his *takeover* of the ad agency. Unwilling to blame himself for the demise of EXSCAPES, he'd decided to exact revenge on the Alexander twins. He'd reasoned that if they no longer believed in his ability to succeed then who else would? Raleigh had also begun to experiment with illegal drugs, which only amplified his already high blood pressure, which ultimately resulted in him experiencing the fatal heart attack.

The entire fiasco was now relegated to the past. Milan and Paris were united in their desire to grow their father's agency. They took advantage of every opportunity to increase their knowledge about the advertising agency business. Paris had even enrolled in some business courses at EMORY UNIVERSITY.

One week ago the ALEXANDER AGENCY had made the final cut on the SOME BODY FITNESS CENTERS ad review. The agency was scheduled to make their final presentation to the advertiser's executive management team in just a few days – right before the Thanksgiving holiday.

Milan and Paris were seated at opposite ends of the long conference table. They were joined by the agency's senior creative team, which consisted of three women and one man.

The senior vice president for creative services was addressing the group. "Well, we already know that they like what we have to offer for their new campaign," she told her colleagues. "But I feel that it is very important that we show our versatility."

"Are you saying that we should deviate from the current campaign?" Paris asked her.

"Exactly! I mean imagine how a whole new campaign will come across to them," she said enthusiastically.

One of the creative directors spoke. "Yeah, I think that would be really cool! It will allow them to see that we don't have all of our eggs in one basket."

Paris nodded towards Milan to seek her input.

"Hey, you guys are the creative geniuses around here. I trust your recommendations," Milan stated.

"We haven't lost an account since you brought us aboard, right?" the senior VP quipped.

"That is true," Paris interjected. "But my only concern is whether or not we have time to come up with a new campaign? I mean we are presenting on Friday,"

"Now, that's where I come in," the only male in the room began. He was a senior copywriter. "You see, the ladies here had already considered the possibility that we would make the final cut, so for the past couple of months I've been working on some ideas."

"You da man, Naoko!" Paris remarked, as she reached across the table and gave him a high-five. The senior copywriter's eyes lit up.

Naoko Jackson was a twenty-nine year-old transplant from a large New York ad agency. After reading stories about the twins in the newspaper and after catching a glimpse of Paris on the TODAY SHOW one morning, he knew then that he had to work at their agency. He didn't think twice about leaving a job that he'd held since graduating college and heading south. He was a single man and there was nothing or no one holding him down in the NYC. His parents, a black father and a Japanese mother, were also supportive of his decision. Of course they lived in nearby South Carolina so it was a little difficult for them not to want their only son close to home.

The day before he left New York, he'd mailed his resume to the ALEXANDER AGENCY. Three days later while he was strolling into their office building, the mail carrier was sliding the ivory-colored envelope that contained his resume into their mailbox on the first floor. An hour later he was sitting in front of the agency's recently hired senior VP for creative services answering her question on why she should hire him.

Having worked on top-notch accounts back in New York, and with an impressive array of creative awards received during his career, Naoko Jackson felt pretty confident that he would be hired as a senior copywriter. And he was. However, not without a slight reduction in salary. But Naoko didn't mind the pay cut. His eyes were on a much bigger prize – a chance to win the heart of the woman whom he'd developed an instant crush on – Paris Alexander.

"Well, let them hear what you've come up with," the senior VP coaxed him, as he'd momentarily slipped into dreamland.

"Uh, yeah, right." He quickly shuffled some papers in front of him. "Um, the idea for this TV commercial is to use the music from the song *'Everybody Plays The Fool'* by *The Main Ingredient*," he began.

Milan and Paris listened with great interest.

"The commercial opens with quick shots of different people with various body types staring at themselves in the mirror. And throughout these shots, the music is playing with the lyrics, *everybody plays the fool sometime . . .*"

Wide grins spread across the twins' face. "I like this idea already," piped Milan.

"Now, just imagine the various body types – an overweight middle-aged guy with a protruding stomach, or a young skinny woman with no behind. Then after a few lines of just "the chorus, the voice-over says, *'don't let your body keep playing you for a fool; get in shape the way every body deserves to get in shape at SOME BODY FITNESS CENTERS'.*"

"I love it!" screamed Milan.

"So do I," echoed Paris. "What's the tagline?"

Naoko glanced at some notes in front of him. "The tagline, which will also be used in print ads, says EVERY BODY CAN BE SOME BODY."

Paris repeated the words quietly to herself. "You know, that's real catchy! I like it!"

Naoko beamed with pride.

"It sounds like a winner!" Milan said.

"That's exactly what we thought when he first ran the idea by us," one of the creative directors spoke.

"Well, we've got about three days to put it all together," Paris mentioned.

Naoko went on to explain that the storyboards for the TV commercial had already been completed. He told the group that he'd also met with Legal to have them go through the proper channels in securing the rights to use the song. Milan and Paris were thoroughly impressed not only with his idea but with his initiative as well.

"Guys, we're talking twenty million in annual billings if we can win this account," Milan reminded them.

"No *if* about it, girl," Paris chided her. "Because *we* are somebody, SOME BODY is ours!"

Joyous laughter filled the room. But it was interrupted when Belinda's voice piped through the telephone console that sat in the middle of the conference table. "Paris?" she called out.

"Yes, Belinda," Paris answered.

"I have a call holding for you."

"Belinda, I'm in a meeting – didn't I tell you that earlier?"

"I know, and I'm sorry to interrupt, but it's your son's school."

Paris peeked at her watch. There was still an hour to go before Tristan's school let out. "Okay, fine. Give me a minute to get back to my office and then transfer it there," she instructed the receptionist. "I should only be gone a minute, guys," she apologized, as she pushed her chair away from the table. As she stood she adjusted the designer skirt that she was wearing, tucked strands of curls behind her diamond-pierced ears, slid her chair back to the table and then gracefully glided from the room.

Naoko Jackson watched her adoringly until her physical presence had disappeared through the door. Although, the mental presence of her that he'd conjured up would linger throughout the afternoon.

CHAPTER
TEN

"**Hello,** Miss Alexander. This is Martha Montgomery calling from THORNHILL CHRISTIAN ACADEMY."

Paris couldn't understand why she always seemed to be *introducing* herself whenever she called. It wasn't as if this was their first conversation. In fact, since the beginning of the school year this past August, she must have fielded some ten to fifteen calls from Tristan's first-grade teacher. And the majority of them had much to do about nothing. "Hi Martha," Paris greeted her, rolling her eyes towards the ceiling. "What can I do for you?"

"Well, it seems our little Tristan was a bit preoccupied at school today," the elderly woman began.

"Really? And how so?"

"Well, he kept touching the hair of the girl that sits in front of him."

"Did he upset the girl?"

"Oh, no. Not at all."

"Did she ask him to stop touching her hair?"

"Well, no. You see, Miss Alexander, actually the student appeared to be ignoring our little Tristan. But from my desk, I could see him putting his hands on her hair. And, well, that is a classroom no-no. All the students know that they must keep their hands to themselves."

Paris could not believe that she'd just been pulled from a campaign meeting to engage in this ridiculous conversation.

In as polite a voice that she could muster, Paris said, "With all due respect, Martha, is this *really* that big of a deal? I mean he's six years old – kids will do these things."

The teacher was taken aback. "Well, it's simply not the kind of behavior that we at Thornhill Christian Academy wishes to condone. Besides, Miss Alexander, need I remind you that this isn't the first conversation that we've had regarding our little Tristan."

"No, as a matter of fact it isn't. And need I remind you that every single conversation has had something to do with your interpretation of my son's behavior."

"Interpretation?"

"Correct. Less than one week into the school year you were complaining to me that Tristan wouldn't sit still at his desk. A week later he was getting in and out of the lunch line. Then he wouldn't stay on his mat at naptime. I mean don't insult my intelligence, Martha. I know where these conversations have been leading!" It was becoming difficult for Paris not to raise her voice.

"Well, now. I must assure you that any communication that I've had with you regarding our little Tris . . ."

"Will you stop referring to him like that!" Paris interrupted her. "He's not *your* little Tristan. He's your *student* and *my* son. I'd very much appreciate it if you'd refer to him by his name and nothing more, nothing less."

"Why, Miss Alexander, there's no need to get upset. I'm simply trying to do what's in the best interest of our . . . err, Tristan, that's all."

"Listen, Martha. That may very well be true. But I do not want to have my child under your daily microscope. Since he entered Thornhill last year there's been one label after another put on him and I will not allow this to continue."

"Oh, no Miss Alexander. We do not place labels on any of our students."

Paris sucked her teeth. "Then stop sending me literature on *classroom behaviors*, and especially stuff about *RITALIN*!" No sooner had Tristan entered kindergarten last year, he'd somehow already been labeled with *learning disabilities* simply because he fidgeted in his seat during class. His teacher at that time had alluded to the possibility that he may have *Attention Deficit Disorder*, or A-D-D. And of course the school wanted to recommend the prescription drug, RITALIN. But little did they know, Paris was already one step ahead of them. With Milan teaching in the public school system, she'd shared with Paris the fact that so many schools across the country were quick to label a student with ADD simply because of perceived learning or behavior problems. Far worse, African-American boys were much more likely to have mind-altering drugs prescribed for them.

"Miss Alexander, any information that we've provided to you with regards to behavior as well as learning problems, were simply done to educate you on what solutions are available to ensure your child's success in the classroom."

Paris was becoming quite fed up with this woman. She was beginning to second-guess her decision to send Tristan to a private school. "Martha, the main reason that I chose to enroll my son at Thornhill is because of the Christ-like environment that you all supposedly fosters."

"Spirituality is very much a part of our curriculum," the teacher was quick to interject.

"Well, since you are obviously not prohibited from praying in school, why not spend more time praying with a student if there's a problem rather than complaining about every little thing that occurs in the classroom to the parent?"

"Oh, the students attend chapel on a daily basis."

"I'm not referring to the students. I'm talking about the faculty and the administrators. It appears that you all do a great job emphasizing the *Christian* aspect in your name as well as your marketing materials, but yet there seems to be little Christian values and principles being practiced "

"Well, I must say that I'm offended by your comments, Miss Alexander."

And you should be, Paris wanted to say. "It is not my intention to offend you, Martha, but to *educate* you on how I believe a so-called *Christian school* should handle matters. The teachers at Thornhill should be praying for their students without ceasing. Not trying to diagnose whether they have ADD or not. And when a problem arises between two students, teach those students how to handle the problem in a Christ-like manner, not by using disciplinary actions that can "be easily found in non-Christian schools."

"Well, I don't set the school's policies, Miss Alexander. I'm only a teacher at Thornhill."

"All I'm saying, Martha, is that I'm sending my son to this school because I want him to get a good education and I want him to do so in a Christian environment."

"And we're happy to have him here! Thornhill has been nominated as a *National School of Excellence* for the past five years consecutively. Our test scores are among the highest within the state."

"Those are noble achievements," Paris acknowledged. "But in all honesty, I'm more concerned about my child getting into the *gates* of Heaven than I am about him getting into the *doors* of Harvard."

"Of course. However, it is imperative that we do strive for academic excellence. On the other hand, if our principles are not agreeable to you, we know that there are plenty of other schools from which you may choose. Although, here at Thornhill we have quite a waiting list."

Paris couldn't believe her arrogance. "I'm fully aware that I can enroll my son wherever I choose. And for the record, I will be giving some serious consideration as to whether or not I want to *keep* him enrolled at Thornhill."

"Why, that's certainly your prerogative, Miss Alexander."

"Yes, it is."

Having said that, Paris ended her phone conversation with the long-winded teacher. She told her that in the future she would prefer that any comments or concerns that she has about Tristan, to send a note home with him or send her an email. She did not want to be pulled away from a meeting at work to discuss matters that the teacher should be capable of handling within her own classroom.

C H A P T E R
ELEVEN

DECEMBER in Atlanta this time around brought some unusually cold temperatures. Even though it was just the first day of the month, the wind was howling louder than a hungry infant. And although the actual temperature was registering at thirty-one degrees, the wind chill made it feel like it was eighteen. Kids around the city were wishing for even an *inch* of snow so that the schools would close. Never mind the fact that they'd just come off their Thanksgiving holiday break.

Milan was standing at her office window deep in thought. If there was one truth that she'd learned about the advertising agency business it was the fact that *you win some* and *you lose some*. Earlier on this Wednesday, they'd received a call from the chief marketing officer at SOME BODY FITNESS CENTERS. The tone of his voice had already indicated the bad news that was to come. The account had been awarded to a rival agency. They had been so sure that they would win the account. She tried not to look at it as though they'd lost twenty million dollars in billings since they never had the account in the first place. But somehow the loss hurt just the same. And it would not have been so difficult to digest if it weren't for the fact that, just two days earlier, their agency was informed that their largest account, CASHMERE COLLINS, a national chain of women's fashion stores, was placing their account up for review. And the kicker? They were not invited to participate! Sixty-five million dollars in billings were about to be taken away from them and they weren't even allowed to defend themselves.

"It's nothing personal," the client had assured them. "We're just ready for a change."

She and Paris had met with Aunt Millie last night at Paris' home and the three of them prayed fervently for God's intervention. The loss of CASHMERE COLLINS was going to mean the loss of fifty-two percent of their annual billings. It would be nearly impossible for the agency to withstand such a devastating blow. And while the impending publicity would undoubtedly be overwhelming, Milan was more concerned about their employees. They were all like a family. She could not bear the thought of any of them having to be let go, especially at *this* time of the year.

A chuckle escaped her as she peered through the window, looking below at the parking lot, and watching with some amusement as a gentleman's hat flew off his head. The gusting winds carried the hat through the air and two rows over where it finally landed on top of an SUV. Milan couldn't quite tell from her view, but it looked like a Chevy Suburban. The poor guy began searching frantically for his hat, unaware of where it had come to rest. She wanted to scream to him where to look, but she realized that her efforts would be futile. And just as he appeared to call off the search, another gust blew the hat from the vehicle causing it to land just a few feet in front of him.

Things always seemed to have a way of working themselves out, she thought to herself.

The buzzing of her telephone disrupted her moment of tranquility. She made her way back to her desk, plopped down into her baby blue leather chair and pressed the button for the *speakerphone*. "Milan Alexander," she answered.

"Hi Milan, it's Blade."

Blade Barnes served as the agency's outside counsel and corporate adviser. At a time when so many others were watching and waiting for her and Paris to fall flat on their faces, Blade has been a staunch supporter. He was a law graduate from STANFORD UNIVERSITY, and after spending a summer clerking for a Judge in Atlanta he'd decided to move to the city upon graduating. He would later land a position as an associate attorney with one of Atlanta's leading law firms. And five years later he'd made partner in the firm, becoming just the third African-American to have such a promotion bestowed upon him.

Blade worked in various areas of corporate law. It was the assignment of the ALEXANDER AGENCY to him that led to his association with Everson Alexander. But three years ago Blade gave up the security and rewards of being a law partner to hang up his own shingle. When he walked away from the law firm, Everson had followed.

"Oh, hi Blade," Milan answered, a lifeless monotone to her voice.

"Is something wrong?" Blade asked. He could tell that she wasn't her usual jubilant self.

"Where do I start?"

"That bad, huh?"

"Worse. We didn't win SOME BODY FITNESS."

"I'm sorry to hear that."

"That wasn't the worst part. CASHMERE COLLINS has placed its account up for review."

Blade exhaled a heavy sigh. "Wow. That's your largest account."

"I know."

"Well, if there's anything that I can do to help you guys prepare for the review I'm willing. I mean don't count on me for any creative ideas, but I'm pretty good at strategizing."

"Thanks, Blade. That's very kind of you to offer. But unfortunately the client did not invite us to participate in the review."

"Are you kidding?"

"I only wish. We're about to looc an account that's over fifty percent of our billings."

"That's going to be catastrophic, to say the least. How much time before the review process?"

"Virtually none. The client wants to have a new agency named before Christmas."

"What! That's less than four weeks away. Do they seriously expect any agency to have a campaign ready to present in such a short period of time?"

"Apparently."

"It makes you wonder if whether or not they'd gotten the ball rolling well before informing you guys."

"Exactly what I was thinking."

Blade stood from his chair and sat on a corner of his desk. "How are you and Paris planning to handle this?"

"Honestly? I have no idea. Paris is meeting with our entire creative team as we speak. I mean the loss of sixty-five million dollars will more than likely cause all sorts of ripple effects. Your top people get nervous and start looking for other opportunities. The other clients begin to wonder if you'll become too distracted by the loss to focus on their account. And the next thing you know we're staring bankruptcy in the face."

"Wow, you have learned a lot about the business over the past year," Blade stated, only half joking. "But I don't believe the situation calls for sackcloth and ashes just yet."

"Well, I'm not sure that I share your belief. But you know what? I can't help but wonder what my dad would do in this situation?"

For a moment Blade recalled to mind the astute Everson Alexander. "I know what he wouldn't do?"

"What's that?"

"Give up. Your father was not only a proud man but also a relentless fighter, Milan. He'd find a way to overcome this minor setback."

"*Minor?*"

"Okay, *major* setback. But irregardless, he'd dig in his heels and prepare to get back into the game."

Milan realized that Blade was absolutely right. She couldn't ever remember a time when her father backed away from a challenge or an obstacle. Even after their mother had abandoned them, her father refused to remarry. And although he eventually filed for divorce, she knew that hope remained alive in his heart that their mother – his wife – would one day return.

"Giving up is not an option for neither myself nor Paris. But we will need some guidance on how to deal with this, Blade."

"Of course. And that's what I'm here for. Say, why don't you let me treat you to dinner tonight and we can brainstorm a bit – two heads are better than one you know?"

"Actually *three* heads if you count Paris."

Blade moved from sitting on the corner of his desk back to his chair. He'd hope to have some one-on-one time with Milan. "Well, we're not talking about a *formal* meeting so really there's no need for Paris to join us. I mean if we just happen to come up with a brilliant idea while savoring our meal, then by all means we'll make sure that she shares equal credit."

Milan considered this for a moment. "I guess that makes sense."

"Good. Why don't I pick you up at home – say around seven-thirty?"

"But you're all the way in downtown. I'd hate for you to have to drive to Roswell just to pick me up. Why . . ."

"It's not a problem," he interrupted. "In fact there's this new steakhouse restaurant in Alpharetta that I've been anxious to try, so that's only a couple of exits north of where you are."

"I think I know the restaurant you're talking about – isn't it on *Old Milton Parkway?*"

"Yeah, it is. But for the life of me I can't remember the name."

"Me either."

"Oh well, it doesn't matter. I'll know it when I get there."

As their call ended, Milan glanced at her watch. It was almost two-thirty. She decided to work until five-thirty and then head home. By the time she navigated her way up GEORGIA 400, she should have enough time to shower and dress before Blade arrived. A nice dinner out would be good for her. It had been quite some time since she'd had a date of any kind. Not that she considered dinner with Blade a *date.* Although the man was very handsome, she knew that their interests were strictly professional. He was their attorney and business adviser. Besides, at forty-one he was *fifteen* years older than her. Not that there was anything wrong with that. If she were interested in someone seriously she'd want him to be much older than her anyway. Older men were not only mature but also stable. At least most of them were. She really had very little interest in the *twenty-somethings* that repeatedly hit on her. Most were trifling, with only one thing on their minds and sadly, their minds constantly on one thing.

CHAPTER
TWELVE

Scotty Sims met Paris Alexander when she was sixteen. Paris had been a cheerleader in high school and Scotty was the football team's quarterback at a rival school. The two had made eye contact during a playoff game one Friday night and became magically attracted to one another. After the game ended, Scotty slipped a piece of paper that contained his phone number to the drop-dead-gorgeous cheerleader. Not long after their first conversation together they'd become a couple. Both were juniors in high school at the time. They would eventually date for the next two years.

Seven months after their high school graduations, Paris became pregnant with Scotty's child. Needless to say, Scotty had freaked out once he learned that he was soon to be a daddy – at the responsible age of nineteen. He was now in his freshman year of college at a top University in Florida, having earned his ticket with a football scholarship.

The news of the pregnancy deeply saddened and disappointed her father and devastated her sister who had cried for weeks. It didn't take long for Scotty to begin questioning whether he was *really* the father. His audacity to raise such a question broke Paris' heart because not only was he the only guy she'd been intimate with, but he was also the only guy that she'd ever dated. The two had harsh words with one another, which ultimately resulted in the break-up of their relationship.

When Milan arrived at her sister's office the door was open. Paris was sitting at her desk like a zombie with her eyes glued to the telephone.

"Girl, you're staring at that phone like it's the answer to all our problems," Milan teased as she walked into the office.

"Hey," Paris responded, rising from her chair to give her sister a warm hug.

"I know you're thinking about how we're going to deal with this crisis, but don't stress too much. We have to trust that everything will be all right," Milan told her.

Paris shook her head. "No, actually for the first time today I wasn't thinking about the agency."

"Well, good for you. I only wish I had a strong distraction to take my mind off this agency."

Paris chuckled. "Trust me, sis. You wouldn't want *this* distraction."

Knowing her twin sister all too well, Milan raised one eyebrow in a questioning slant. "Okay, what's going on?" she asked, walking over and closing the door. She then grabbed her sister by the hand and led her to the sofa. "Talk to me, Paris."

Paris allowed her head to drop as she considered whether or not she wanted to discuss the matter. Milan took her finger and gently lifted her sister's chin. Her own heart began to ache as she observed the fallen features displayed on her sister's face.

"I just got off the phone with Scotty," she said softly.

Milan blinked with surprise. "Scotty Sims?"

Paris nodded.

Milan fanned the air with her hand to show her disgust. "You know, I'm a little surprised that he actually waited this long to contact you."

"Yeah, me too."

"I mean you know he had to have read about us over the past year inheriting the agency."

"Oh, I'm sure he did."

"So, what did his trifling behind want?"

Paris stood from the sofa and sauntered around her office. "He wants to meet with me this evening."

"Meet with you! For what, Paris?"

"He said he misses his son."

Milan leaped from the sofa. "You have got to be kidding me!"

"That's what he says."

"Paris, Scotty doesn't care anything about Tristan! I doubt if he even remember the boy's name!"

"He doesn't."

Milan smacked Paris' desk as she walked by it. "Unbelievable! He sees him once, and even that was six months after he was born, and now all of a sudden he wants to talk about his son?"

"Don't worry, girl. I'm not buying that garbage he's trying to sell."

"Well, that's good to hear. So, what else did he have to say?" Milan was curious. The two of them sat down on the sofa again.

"A lot," Paris began, as she shared her earlier conversation.

During his sophomore year in college Scotty had suffered a knee injury early into the football season which had sidelined him for the remainder of the season. Distraught over the injury, he began to drink heavily and hang with the wrong crowd. He eventually dropped out of college altogether. Unbeknownst to Paris, he'd moved back to the Atlanta area three years ago. She asked him why he hadn't contacted her before now, especially if he supposedly had any concern about his son. Scotty had told her that he was living with another woman at time who wasn't aware that he'd fathered a child a few years prior. He has since fathered two additional children by two different women.

Paris knew without a doubt that he had *loser*, with a capital L, written all over his forehead. He wasn't supporting his other two kids and yet he tried to convince her that he wanted to get to know Tristan, whom he kept referring to as 'the lil' dude' because he couldn't remember his name. She asked him if he had a job and without hesitating he said 'no', but that he was "working on it."

"Sis, I'm so glad that you didn't agree to meet with him. He hasn't been in your life for the past six years and you certainly don't need him now – in your life or Tristan's," Milan stated.

"I have absolutely no desire to see Scotty Sims," Paris assured her sister. "I remember when I first told daddy that I was pregnant and that Scotty was the father. And how daddy wanted to rip Scotty to pieces . . ."

"Yes, and how you defended his no good self," Milan interrupted.

"Yeah, I know. If only I had listened when daddy told me that he didn't think I should be dating Scotty. As it turns out daddy was right."

"Daddy was right about a lot of things," Milan said, wrapping her arm around Paris and pulling her close.

"I miss him so much, Milan."

"I do too."

For a moment neither of them uttered another word. It was just after five o'clock and most of the employees had already departed for the day. A few voices could be heard here and there outside Paris' office, but for the most part the silence around them was soothing.

"You know, we haven't heard from that detective in a while," Paris said, breaking the silence.

"I know. They probably won't ever find out who those carjackers were. I mean it was late at night and the one witness who did see it couldn't really identify those thugs."

Paris said, "Didn't the witness tell the police that once the two guys had pulled daddy from the car that he seemed to be urging them to just take the car?"

Milan took in a deep sigh as she fought to control her emotions. "Yes. But they shot him anyway. Twice in the head."

Paris covered her mouth to try and muffle the sobs that had overtaken her. "They didn't have to kill him!"

Milan tried to comfort her sister, all the while fighting her own streaming tears. "Daddy's in a better place now. We have to take comfort in that."

"I know that, but it's not fair that those two thugs are still out there roaming the streets!" Paris said through her cries.

Milan shook her head, a pained expression blanketing her face. "They'll get theirs – eventually."

"The police thought that they would at least find his car abandoned somewhere," Paris said, pulling a Kleenex from the box on the coffee table and then drying her eyes. She pulled another one and handed it to Milan.

Milan dabbed the corners of her eyes. "Daddy was so happy when he'd bought that car."

"Yeah, he was. And I was happy for him too. I mean he'd been driving that Lincoln Town Car for so long!"

Milan chuckled. "I know. Remember how we would always tease him about how small he looked driving that *yacht*!"

Everson Alexander had only been five-foot-six.

Paris' eyes suddenly brimmed with an unmistakable joy. "He took the teasing in stride, though. "

"Of course. That's just how daddy was. But that white Lexus LS430 was definitely the right car for him!"

"It sure was! And I remember that Fourth of July before he died when he'd taken Tristan to the store with him and how Tristan had taken a red ink pen and scribbled *grandpa* on the back of the headrest of daddy's seat."

Milan laughed. "I remember that. We both thought that Tristan was about to get the spanking of his little life."

"Yeah, but daddy just laughed and patted Tristan on the head telling him how good of a speller he was."

"He sure did. And he wouldn't even let you clean it off! He said that it was his grandson's signature mark and that it wasn't going to hurt the car."

Paris closed her eyes briefly, trying to recapture the spirit of her father's kindness and gentleness.

Milan, noticing the time, said, "Sis, I've got to get up out of here."

"Where you running off to?"

"Blade is picking me up later for dinner."

Paris' eyebrows arched. Giving her sister a critical squint she said, "Oh really? Is this a business dinner?"

Milan emitted a nervous chuckle. "Of course. I spoke with him earlier this afternoon about our impending troubles and he suggested that we get together for dinner and brainstorm."

"And you didn't think that maybe I should be part of this brainstorming session?"

Milan fanned the air with her hand. "Sis, it's not that big of a deal."

"You know the man's in love with you, Milan."

"Says who?"

"Me. And I know what I'm talking about so don't try and act all naïve."

"Paris, Blade Barnes is not interested in me. At least not like *that*."

"Humph. I wouldn't be so sure about that. And it's kind of ironic too."

"Ironic?"

Paris walked over to her desk and pretended to be searching for some particular papers. "Well, you know Aunt Millie has a crush on the man."

This was certainly news to Milan. "Aunt Millie? A crush?"

"Don't be too surprised, girl. She's only fifty-six. She can still get her groove on if she chooses."

"I'm not surprised. It's just that . . . well, Aunt Millie is fifteen years older than Blade."

"And you're fifteen years younger!" Paris was quick to point out.

"I know. I mean I'm not hung up on age and all that, but I just thought . . . well, does Blade know?"

"I doubt it. Aunt Millie's too shy to say anything."

"Wait a minute! How do you know who Blade's in love with and who Aunt Millie has a crush on?"

"You know I'm right, Milan. Besides, as far as the crush thing, Aunt Millie told me that herself."

"Really? And why would she tell you and not me too?"

"Well, it wasn't like she called a meeting with me or something just to say that she had a crush on the man. We were simply talking one day and I had brought up Blade's name and I noticed how her eyes lit up. Well, you know me, I put her through my twenty questions and that's how I found out."

Milan was taken aback. "So, did she say if it was a serious crush or was it more of an admiration for him?"

Paris laughed at her sister's behavior. "Listen to yourself! If things are only business between you and Blade then why does it matter to you how Aunt Millie feels about him?"

Milan gave her sister a polite punch on the shoulder. "I'm just curious, that's all."

"Curious or a little jealous?"

"Paris, you need to quit!"

"Hey, I'm only asking!"

Milan decided to flip the script. "You're a fine one to talk."

"What's that supposed to mean?"

"It means that instead of you worrying about my love life, you better be keeping your eye on Naoko Jackson."

Paris erupted in laughter. "Naoko! Oh, Milan please! Don't even try and go there."

"That guy is absolutely crazy about you, Paris."

Paris cupped her hand to her ear. "Hello! I'm Naoko's boss, okay?"

"So what. It's not the first time an employee has fallen in love with his boss."

"Okay, Milan. First of all, Naoko is not in love with me. And I certainly am not in love with him. So, you might as well stop trying to make something up just to deflect attention from you and Blade."

"I guess time will tell," Milan smirked.

"Yeah, I guess it will."

The twins continued to chide one another before Milan decided to call it a day. Both were glad to have had some time to forget, for a while at least, about the agency's crisis that was looming on the horizon.

Paris realized that she also needed to be leaving. Her son's Nanny attended Bible classes on Wednesday nights so she needed to hurry home to relieve her. As she drove home she couldn't help but think about her earlier conversation with Scotty. The last thing she needed right now was drama from him. And while she was somewhat saddened by how his life had turned out, she knew that it was not her responsibility. He was a grown man. He could take care of himself. And she was not about to let him try and use *her* son as a way to get back into her life.

Paris put in *The Diary of Alicia Keys* CD and pressed the button for selection number two – *Karma*. She turned up the volume as she merged onto the highway. As she listened to Alicia belt out the soulful lyrics it was difficult to ignore how much they spoke to her. Their meaning was undeniable.

"Sing it, girlfriend," Paris whispered, bobbing her head.

. . . *What goes around, comes around.*

CHAPTER
THIRTEEN

Blade Barnes couldn't help but feel as if he were a teenager on a first date. With Milan Alexander sitting like a princess in the passenger seat of his Range Rover, it was very difficult for him to keep his eyes focused on the road, or anything else for that matter.

It was just past seven-thirty when they exited off GEORGIA HIGHWAY 400 onto Old Milton Parkway. Traffic was moving about as well as could be expected for a Wednesday evening.

"What CD is that?" Milan asked. She'd been curious since Blade had popped it in, but had tried to figure out on her own who the singer was.

"Joss Stone," Blade answered, checking his mirror before changing to the left lane.

Milan wasn't familiar with the artist. "It really sounds good!"

"Yeah, I like her. I just happened to come across it at the store and I had a chance to listen to a few tracks at the store and I must say that I was quite impressed. And can you believe that she's only *sixteen*?"

"Sixteen? With a soulful voice like that?"

Blade nodded. "I know. It's incredible! She's from England," he added.

"I will definitely have to pick this one up myself," Milan remarked, tapping her heels to the beat of the track, *Fell In Love With A Boy*.

Blade made the turn into the restaurant's parking lot.

"I heard about this place," Milan said, noticing the name on the restaurant – CORUSCATE.

"Yeah, a colleague of mine lives in this area and he and his wife had dinner here a couple of weeks ago and they loved it."

Blade pulled into a parking space that was just a few paces from the front door. He shut off the engine and darted around the car to open the door for Milan. She thanked him for his courtesy.

Their entrance into the restaurant was captivating as they made their way through sparkling lights that led to a three-story foyer. A polite hostess welcomed and greeted them warmly. They chose a comfortable semi-circular booth.

"This place is absolutely beautiful," Milan said as her eyes admired the plush decor.

"I'm glad you like it," Blade replied.

After they'd been seated a courteous waiter came and took their order for drinks. They both selected a glass of white Zinfandel. By the time the waiter returned with the drinks, they were ready to order their dinner. Milan chose the crawfish fettuccini served in a tomato butter sauce with green peppers and onions. Blade decided on the roasted baby back ribs, which were served with a sweet potato salad.

"So, did you have a pretty good afternoon?" Blade asked, taking a sip from his glass.

Milan tossed her hair over her shoulder. "Actually it was okay. I mean nothing eventful. Paris told me that her meeting with the creative team went okay."

"Just okay?"

"Well, I guess when you're being told to prepare for a major client loss there's not a whole lot to get excited about."

"Yeah, I suppose you're right." Blade took another sip. He wasn't quite sure how to broach this next subject. "You know, Milan, there is one option that you guys can consider."

She took a sip from her wine glass. "Hey, I'm all ears!"

"Okay. But first you have to promise not to chop my head off for saying this . . ."

"I wouldn't dream of it."

He smiled at her. "Well, considering the negative financial impact that the loss of CASHMERE COLLINS is going to bring "to the agency, finding a suitable merger partner might be an option to consider," Blade stated.

Milan's face became drawn and pinched. She took two successive sips from her wine glass.

Blade hoped that he hadn't insulted her in any way. "Hey, it's just one of many options, okay? Don't fret over it."

"I totally understand. I mean Paris and I will have to decide something very soon. And I have come to understand that mergers are the only means sometimes by which a company can survive."

Blade flashed her a knowing smile as he reached across the table and rested his hand atop hers. "You're not alone in this, Milan."

She appreciated his assurance. "Thanks. The thing is . . . well, the thought of giving control of my father's agency to someone else is . . . well, it's just heartbreaking."

"I know. That is why I will do everything that I can to make certain that it is the absolute last option."

Milan began to twirl a strand of her hair. "Where do we even begin to look for a merger partner?"

Blade cleared his throat. "Well, a friend of mine is an investment banker on Wall Street. Let me speak with him and see what he recommends."

"All right."

"In the mean time, you guys just keep your heads together. I mean who knows – maybe you'll land enough business to replace CASHMERE COLLINS."

Milan shook her head. "No, not within the time frame that we're under. Six months down the line, maybe. Right now we have no new business pitches scheduled. The loss of CASHMERE COLLINS will impact our bottom line immediately."

"Yeah, I suppose you're right," Blade acknowledged. He decided that it was time to shift the conversation away from business. "You know something?"

"What?"

"Most of what I've learned about you lately I've learned from the media. Why don't you tell me about the *real* Milan Alexander?" he said in a teasing manner.

She could feel herself blushing. "Oh, no! I am such a boring person! I don't know much about *you*, Mr. Barnes?"

Blade smiled at her sheepishly. "Trust me – lawyers can be quite boring too!"

"Well, then don't tell me about Blade Barnes *the lawyer*. Tell me about Blade Barnes *the gentleman*."

Now it was his turn to blush. And Milan knew that he was doing just that as she stared dreamily across the table at him. She began to notice features about his appearance that she hadn't really given much attention to before. His hair was cut evenly on all sides and neatly trimmed. And while she adored a moustache on a man, Blade didn't need one to accentuate his chiseled bronze face. It was obvious that he took good care of his skin. Without hesitation she would have guessed his age to be a few years younger than his actual forty-one. He was of average build and height. And she was yet to see the man without a suit – a designer one at that. Admittedly, she was very attracted to the distinguish manner about him. Even the designer fragrance that emanated through her nostrils when she'd entered his Range Rover was a scent that would undoubtedly linger with her long after the evening had ended.

"So, you consider me a gentleman, huh?"

"You've been nothing less."

He grinned like a Cheshire cat, readily displaying his pearly whites. "Thank you, Milan. It is my intention to provide you with a wonderful evening, full of both food and delightful conversation."

"Speaking of conversation, I believe you were about to tell me about yourself – the *gentleman*?"

"Uh . . . where do I start? I mean, what do you want to know? Ask me anything you like."

Milan shrugged her shoulders. "Just tell me."

"Okay, okay. I'll give you the *Reader's Digest* version."

"All right."

"Let's see, I'm forty-one years *young*. I was born in Louisville, Kentucky but grew up out in California. I have an older sister and a younger brother. I went to undergrad school at UC-BERKELEY, attended law school at STANFORD. I married when I was nineteen, while at UC. Moved to Atlanta after law school. Divorced at age thirty-one. I have a seventeen year-old son, whom I love dearly. My ex-wife and I "have no bitterness between us and are quite amicable." He paused a moment, tapping his index finger against the table. "What else . . . oh, and I love golf, going to the movies and I have been known to pick up a good book every now and then."

Listening to him speak drew her in even more. She found herself leaning into the table. Whether it was the effects of the Zinfandel, she wasn't sure. And the ironic thing was the fact that she'd had conversations with Blade Barnes numerous times over the past year.

"It's hard to believe that you have a seventeen year-old," she said with a smile.

"Why is that?"

"Well, I guess because you don't look old enough."

He chuckled. "If you're trying to win me over with compliments this evening you can stop trying, Milan. I mean you had me when you agreed to this dinner."

She blushed again.

The waiter stopped by their table and informed them that their dinner would be brought out shortly. He refilled both their wine glasses before leaving them alone again.

"If I'm not being too nosy, may I ask why you got a divorce?"

Blade took a long swallow. "That's a fair question. And I could answer it with the usual ones – 'it just wasn't working', 'we grew apart' or 'I wanted something more'. But the truth of the matter is that we had a very happy twelve year marriage."

Milan drained more of her wine. After setting down her glass, her fingers formed a steeple and her expression became one of puzzlement. "So, how does a *happy* twelve year marriage suddenly end in divorce?"

For the first time, Milan could see sadness in his eyes as he contemplated an answer. She realized that it must have been difficult for him. Part of her regretted having put him in this situation.

"Let's just say that *I* thought it was a happy twelve year-marriage. But when your wife gives her affections to another man . . . well," his voice trailed off as he brought his glass to his lips. As he tilted it forward she watched as the soothing liquid flowed from the glass, hopefully comforting him.

"She cheated on you?" Milan was almost afraid to ask.

Blade exhaled deeply. "Let's just say that it was time to put a *period* at the end of the relationship – not a *comma*, not a *semi-colon*, not a *dash*. A period."

This time Milan stretched her hand across the table and took hold of his, giving it a gentle squeeze. "I'm sorry," she whispered.

"Don't be. It's been ten years. She's moved on. And me? Well, I'm getting there."

"I think you'll be okay."

"Yeah, I know I will. I mean with the grace and strength of God behind me how can I not be?"

She was intrigued that he was one who expressed his faith in God. "Blade, are you a deeply religious person?"

"Well, I don't quite know what you mean by *deeply religious*, but I have been baptized for the forgiveness of my sins. And while I don't claim to be without sin, I try and live according to the Father's commands and teachings."

"Which church do you attend?"

"Actually, I don't attend as often as I perhaps should, but when I do I worship at this non-denominational congregation over in Marietta."

"Really? Well, I'd love to visit with you sometime."

He smiled at her. "I think I would enjoy that."

The waiter arrived with their entrees. Both of them were quite anxious to sink their teeth into the meal. After everything had been set before them Blade offered a prayer of thanks for the food and then they went about devouring the delicious spread.

CHAPTER
FOURTEEN

ADVERTISING AGE magazine ran the story one week before Christmas. CASHMERE COLLINS had completed its ad review process within an astonishing three weeks. The account had been awarded to a Chicago agency. Annual billings for the ALEXANDER AGENCY had officially dropped from $125 million to some $60 million.

Most of the agency's employees were trying their best to proceed in a business-as-usual mindset, but it was quite clear that they were walking around on eggshells. Milan and Paris were really concerned about their key people, who at this point, were basically low hanging fruit ripe for picking.

"Your voice-mail message sounded urgent," Paris said as she entered Milan's office.

"Please close the door," Milan instructed her.

Paris closed the door and then took a seat in one of the two chairs that sat in front of her sister's desk. "I hope there's not another bombshell or something," Paris stated.

Milan placed the cap on the pen that she'd been holding and let it fall to her desk pad. "We could have a *White Knight*," she told Paris.

Paris gave her sister a guarded look. "Are you saying that you've found a merger partner?"

"Actually, it seems they found us. I just got off the phone with a guy named *Sydney Salinas*."

"Never heard of him," Paris said, crossing her legs.

"Neither have I!" Milan said, rising from her chair. She walked around her desk and sat in the chair that was adjacent to where Paris was seated. "But we're both familiar with his ad agency – SALINAS WORLDWIDE."

"That huge Hispanic agency?"

Milan nodded. "After my phone conversation with him I did a quick check in the *Agency Redbook* and they bill around three hundred million a year!"

Skepticism crept over Paris' face. "Why would an agency their size want to merge with us? Especially after we've just lost a sixty-five million dollar account?"

"Well, they wouldn't actually be merging with us," Milan explained. "They want to buy us."

Paris sprung for her chair like she'd been sitting on a hot stove. "Milan no! This is daddy's agency! How can you even consider selling?"

Milan walked over to her sister and grabbed her by the hand. "Paris, just hear me out, okay?" She led her sister back to her chair. They both sat. "First, let me assure you that until my conversation with Blade three weeks ago, neither merging nor selling were even an option. But you and I both know that we've got to do something or else there won't be an agency at all. Granted, we're putting all decisions off until January, but that's right around the corner."

"I hear what you're saying, Milan. But I'd rather deal with the difficulty in letting some employees ago as opposed to selling the agency. I mean who's to say that once they bought us they're not going to clean house anyway?"

"This is what I'm trying to tell you. Yes, SALINAS WORLDWIDE wants to buy us, but they are willing to allow us to operate autonomously. Think about it, Paris! This could be a huge blessing! I mean, you and I would remain as co-CEOs and we would maintain control of day-to-day operations of the agency – including hiring decisions."

Paris shook her head. "Milan, doesn't this sound just too good to be true?"

Milan hesitated. "Well, maybe a little. But hey, we will have Blade and his people check everything out thoroughly before we sign off on anything."

Paris remained skeptical. "Milan, I know we're familiar with "the *name* of their agency, but we don't really know who they are. I mean this *Sydney* guy; he's not the head of the agency is he? Because I thought SALINAS was run by a woman."

"My thoughts exactly. But he shared with me that it is his mother, *Mirabella Salinas*, who heads the agency. Sydney is the executive vice president for strategic planning."

"I see. Well, considering that they specialize in marketing to Latinos, I can understand how they might want to acquire an agency that specialized in marketing to African-Americans," Paris said.

"Which is also why I think they're willing to allow us to operate independently. I mean it only makes sense."

"Yeah, but I still can't understand why they wouldn't go after some of the bigger African-American agencies like BURRELL?"

Milan fanned the air with her hand. "Who knows, Paris? Maybe they attempted to and BURRELL simply wasn't interested."

"Possibly."

Milan could see the apprehension displayed throughout her sister's face. "We've been praying about the agency's situation for a while now, Paris. I'm not saying that SALINAS WORLDWIDE is the answer to our prayers, but we at least have to pursue this."

Paris threw her head back against the chair and stared at the ceiling. "You're right, girl. So, what's the next step?"

"Well, Sydney says that he'll plan to fly over from Dallas the first week of the New Year to meet with us. I told him that I would have our attorney present, but he said that would happen at a later meeting. He only wants to meet with the two of us."

"Why just us?"

"He wants us to have an opportunity to learn about them and ask any questions. I guess you can call it an introductory meeting. I mean if we don't like him there'd be no point in moving forward, right?"

Paris shook her head. "I guess. Will this *Mirabella* person be coming as well?"

Milan pursed her lips. "You know, I'm not sure. I mean he didn't say one way or the other."

"That's really not a big deal. If SALINAS WORLDWIDE does buy us then I'm sure we'll eventually meet Mirabella Salinas," Paris remarked.

"No doubt," Milan agreed.

With Christmas arriving on Saturday, the twins decided that they'd work until Wednesday and then close the offices until after the New Year's holiday. Both had originally planned to take the entire week before Christmas off, but after learning of their impending account loss they realized that their presence at the office would be needed.

"You are coming to Aunt Millie's for Christmas Eve dinner, aren't you?" Paris asked.

"Of course," Milan replied.

"Good because she's really looking forward to having us over. And by the way, she also invited Blade."

"Blade?" Milan was surprised.

"Yeah. Apparently his son is spending the holidays with his mom and stepfather so she didn't want him to be alone."

"Really?"

"Hey, don't get all bent out of shape! She knows that you and Blade had this big dinner out and that he might be interested in you on more than just a professional level . . ."

"How does she know all that?" Milan interrupted.

"Girl, I'm a *peacemaker*, okay? And listening to how you just went on and on about that man after you two had dinner, well, I wasn't about to let Aunt Millie pursue something that probably had no chance of happening."

Milan reached over and threw her arms around Paris. "You are such a sweet sister!"

"Yeah, yeah, yeah. Tell me something I don't already know."

The twins engaged one another in conversation for a few more minutes before Paris headed next door to her office. She couldn't stop thinking about Milan's conversation with SALINAS WORLDWIDE. Maybe this was the blessing that God had sent them. For all of their sakes she certainly hoped that SALINAS truly was their *White Knight*.

Paris didn't even want to consider the possibility that this Sydney Salinas guy could very well turn out to be nothing more than a *Trojan horse*.

CHAPTER
FIFTEEN

Soulful Christmas music played softly in the background as Paris looked over budget reports for the upcoming year that had been submitted by the agency's various department heads. And unless a deal was struck with their new suitor next month, she realized that not only would the budgets that had been submitted become history, but that those who submitted them were also in jeopardy of becoming *past* employees.

She glanced at her watch. It was two o'clock. Most of their employees had already left for the Christmas break. It was a somber time for them all. With much reluctance, she and Milan had decided to cancel their annual Christmas party. There had been some small departmental celebrations, but nothing that was agency-wide.

Just a couple more hours and she'd be out the door as well. She had no intentions of even coming back to her office until January third of the New Year. The end of *2003* could not come fast enough. Ever since the Raleigh Robinson nightmare, things seemed to go downhill. There had been no warning signs that they would lose CASHMERE COLLINS as a client and they certainly would have bet the farm that they would win SOME BODY FITNESS CENTERS.

She wondered what *2004* had in store. Would they really become part of a much larger agency? Or would there be more surprises – that *other* shoe perhaps just waiting to drop?

The ringing of Paris' phone interrupted her thoughts. The receptionist had been allowed to leave at noon so that she could catch a flight home to spend the holidays with her parents in Michigan. But before leaving, Belinda had programmed the switchboard so that the calls were sent directly to each person's office.

"This is Paris," she answered.

"Hi, Paris. It's Nikki."

Nikki was her son's fulltime Nanny. Paris had hired her soon after learning that she would become co-CEO of their father's ad agency. The eighteen year-old woman had just graduated high school at the time and had not decided if she wanted to attend college or not. Paris had found out about her through an acquaintance. Nikki was great with kids and she absolutely adored Tristan. And due to Paris' hectic schedule, the Nanny also lived with them in her three-bedroom townhouse.

"Hi, Nikki. What's up?"

"I just wanted you to know that Tristan's father just dropped off a bunch of gifts. Where should I put them?"

Scotty had begged her to let him take Tristan to the mall with him to buy Christmas gifts. But Paris wasn't having any of that. Since his initial phone call several weeks ago, he'd been calling her practically non-stop inquiring about Tristan. So much so that it had begun to get on Paris' nerves. She agreed to let him buy Tristan some gifts for Christmas. But she was adamant that she would not tell her son that he was his father. Before that, she'd allowed him to come by the house once to see Tristan. He was introduced simply as 'a friend of mommy's'. The entire visit lasted no more than ten minutes. Mostly because that was about as much time that Paris could stand being around him, and partly because he'd been driven over to her house by a female friend who had waited impatiently out in the car.

"Just put the gifts in the closet in my bedroom, Nikki," Paris told her. "Tristan didn't see them did he?"

"No. I was able to distract him while Scotty went out to the car to get them."

"Good. How many were there?" she was curious.

"Four boxes. Actually four *large* boxes," Nikki emphasized.

"Where are the boxes now?" Paris asked.

"In my bedroom."

"Okay. Well, when you think he's not looking you can take them to my room and put them in the closet."

"All right."

"How's he been today?"

"We've been having a great time! I took him to MCDONALD'S earlier for lunch and he got a chance to play on the indoor playground."

"I'll bet he enjoyed that!"

"Um hum. I think it tired him out too because he fell asleep in the car on the way home."

Paris laughed. "That's funny because just the other day he was trying to convince me that since he was six years old now he was *too old* to be taking naps!"

"He's definitely a character," Nikki said, chuckling herself. "Oh, by the way. Scotty had asked if Tristan could go out and sit in his car for a minute. And . . ."

Paris interrupted her, emitting a startled gasp. "Nikki don't tell me you allowed him to be alone with Tristan!"

"I'm sorry, Paris," she offered. "But Tristan kept whining to go out and look at the car and Scotty said that it would only be for a minute and I swear that's all the time it was!"

Paris closed her eyes. She trapped the phone's receiver between her ear and her shoulder as she began to massage her temples with her fingers. "It doesn't matter how long it was for, Nikki. I specifically told you not to let him take Tristan from the house and not to leave him alone with my son! Who knows what Scotty said to him out in the car!"

Nikki's voice had degenerated into a childish whimper. "Paris, I stood at the front door the whole time and watched them, I swear! Tristan did nothing but play in the car. I mean at first he was sitting in the driver's seat and pretended like he was driving the car. Then he hopped in the back seat and that's where he stayed. Scotty didn't even get in the car with him – he rolled the windows down and was leaning his head through the passenger door just watching Tristan play."

Paris sighed. "Nikki, do you remember the conversation I first had with you about Scotty?"

"Um hum."

"Then you know how important this is to me!"

"I said I'm sorry, Paris. It won't happen again."

"It better not! In fact, from now on I don't even want you to open the door for Scotty if I'm not there, is that clear?"

"Um hum."

"Where's Tristan now?"

"Playing in his room."

"Put him on the phone, please."

Paris waited while Nikki set down the phone and called out for Tristan to come here. He bounded from his room and raced down the stairs. "You call me, Nikki?" he wanted to know as he skipped the last three steps by jumping over them. "Tristan, don't jump off the stairs like that," Nikki scolded him. "You could get hurt!"

"Uh unh," Tristan said, shaking his head. "I'm tough!"

"Here," Nikki said, handing the phone to him. "Your mom wants to talk to you."

"Mommy!" he screamed, even before he had the phone up to his ear and mouth.

Paris' heart swelled. "How's my baby?"

"I'm *six* mommy!" he quickly shouted. "Babies are *five!*"

Paris stifled a laugh. "Mommy forgot. So, how's my big strong boy?"

"He's good!"

"Are you having a fun day?"

"I'm in my room watching *Sponge Bob!*"

"You are! Well, maybe we can watch some of it together when I get home."

"Okay."

"Mommy will be home in just a little while."

"Okay. And guess what mommy?"

"What baby . . . um, *big boy?*"

"Mister Scotty came over today and I got to sit in his car!"

"You did?"

"Yeah, and it was a really cool car!"

"I'm sure it was."

"It's just like grandpa's! But his *Exis* is black."

Paris laughed. "Tristan, it's *Lexus.*" She spelled it out for him and got him to repeat the name back to her. "You got it!"

"And guess what else mommy?"

"Okay, Tristan. Tell mommy one more thing then I have to go."

Just then she heard the phone hit the floor with a loud crash. "Sorry, mommy. I dropped the phone."

"It's okay. Tristan, let mommy speak back to Nikki, okay?"

"But I didn't get to tell you," he whined into the phone.

"I'm on my way home so you can tell me when I get there, okay?"

"Okay. Bye mom," he said with a wounded tone in his voice. He handed the phone to Nikki and trudged over to the stairs and sat on the bottom step with his chin resting in the palm of his hands.

"I'm back," Nikki answered again.

"Hey, I'm about to finish up here and then I should be home within the next two hours."

"All right."

"Listen, I know you've made plans to spend the holidays with your family, but I want to give you something before you leave tomorrow, okay?"

"That's so nice, Paris. But remember I told you that I don't have to leave tomorrow. I can work through Christmas Eve."

"Absolutely not, Nikki. Tristan and I will be fine. Besides we're having dinner with my Aunt on Christmas Eve and you need to spend time with your family as well."

"I know. But it's not like I have to travel out of town or something. They just live right over in Duluth!"

"Don't try and argue with me, young lady."

"Oh, all right. I'll leave tomorrow."

After their call ended, Nikki replaced the receiver and walked over and sat beside Tristan. "Hey, big guy. Don't look so sad."

Tristan lifted his head and stared at Nikki with puppy dog eyes. "Mommy didn't let me tell her," he mumbled.

Nikki wrapped an arm around him and scooted him closer to her. "Your mommy has had a very busy day. And she's been so busy so that she can hurry home to spend time with you!"

"But I only wanted to tell her about the Exis, I mean Lexus."

"Well, how about you tell me?"

His little face was etched in disappointment. "But I really wanted to tell mommy."

"Tell her what?"

"I told you! About the Lexus!"

"Well, what about the Lexus?"

"I wrote grandpa's name on it!"

Nikki was confused. "Tristan, what are you talking about?"

"See, you don't understand. I guess because you wasn't there when it happened," he said frustrated.

"When what happened?"

"Never mind," he told her.

"C'mon, Tristan. You can share it with me. I'm your friend aren't I?"

He shook his head.

"Well, friends listen to what each other have to say. So, I want to listen to what you have to say."

"Okay, okay," he said begrudgingly. "When I was four years old, my grandpa took me to the store with him one day. And I was sitting in the back seat of his black Lexus. And while he was driving the car, I spelled his name on the back of his seat with my ink pen."

"Did you get in trouble?"

"Uh unh. Grandpa said that I was a good speller!"

"Well, I think that you're a great speller."

"Mommy wanted to wash it off but grandpa wouldn't let her do it. He said he like it and it could stay right there!"

Nikki smiled at him. "I bet your grandpa was a very special man."

He shook his head again. "And now mommy's friend has a car just like grandpa's with my spelling on it!"

"Well good for you!" Nikki told him. "All right, big guy. Let's go upstairs and take a look at your room. We don't want it to be all messy when your mom gets home."

"Last one up the stairs is a rotten egg!" he shouted, bolting up the stairs, easily beating Nikki to the top.

When she finally arrived at the top of the steps she tackled him in the hallway. "Since you cheated, big guy, I'm going to tickle you silly!" He screamed with laughter as she began to work her fingers all around his tummy.

CHAPTER
SIXTEEN

SALINAS WORLDWIDE ranked as the largest advertising agency in the U.S. that specialized in marketing to Latinos. Their annual billings topped *$330 million* and their employees numbered over two hundred and sixty. Based in Dallas, they also had offices in Miami, Los Angeles, New York, Puerto Rico and Venezuela.

Fifty-three year-old *Mirabella Salinas* had taken control of the ad agency some twenty-one years ago from her husband, Carlos, who died from a brain tumor. They had a four year-old son at the time, Sydney.

Sydney Salinas had been groomed very early on to one day share the agency's reins with his mother. She began teaching him about the advertising business when he was just twelve years old. He would eventually receive an MBA from NORTHWESTERN UNIVERSITY. And now, at the age of twenty-five, he was the agency's EVP for strategic planning.

As he gazed out the window from his first-class seat aboard the AMERICAN AIRLINES plane, Sydney's anticipation grew as they prepared for landing. He was quite anxious to meet Milan and Paris Alexander.

Less than two years after graduating NORTHWESTERN, his mother had assigned a special project to him. Like a lot of people in the industry, she'd read about the Alexander twins being thrust at the helm of their father's ad agency after his tragic death. She'd asked Sydney to put together a file on the

ALEXANDER AGENCY and monitor their progress. When it was learned that the twins' agency was about to lose a significant portion of their annual billings, Mirabella Salinas began to entertain the idea of an acquisition.

Sydney felt a slight jolt as the plane's wheels made contact with the runway. A smile spread across his face. He hated to fly. Yet, there was always a sense of relief when the plane landed. The *takeoffs* terrified him the most. Mainly because he was afraid of heights and the idea of leaving the ground simply didn't sit too well with him. On the other hand, the *landings* brought a certain rush of excitement to him because he knew that he would be getting closer and closer to the ground as the plane descended from the sky.

The weather was mild on this Tuesday afternoon as he exited the HARTSFIELD-JACKSON INTERNATIONAL AIRPORT in Atlanta. A limo driver had been awaiting his arrival at BAGGAGE CLAIM. There were several other drivers there as well, all holding up signs with the names of passengers whom they were obviously not familiar with. Sydney had recognized the driver holding a sign with his name on it right away.

The limo driver opened the back door to the stretched vehicle as Sydney climbed inside. He'd ridden in limousines several times before, but never alone. It almost seemed ridiculous that this huge car, which could easily seat ten people, had been sent just for one person. But it was courtesy of the Alexander twins, so he chose not to complain.

After weaving his way through the airport's congestion, the driver picked up speed and made his way onto the interstate. Sydney took notice as they drove under the sign directing them towards I-85 NORTH.

He retrieved his black MOTOROLA MPX-200 cell phone from the breast pocket of his suit jacket and decided to give them a call to let them know that he'd arrived safely and was en route to their offices. He flipped the cover and only had to press a single digit on the keypad. The ALEXANDER AGENCY had already been programmed into his speed dial – several months earlier.

CHAPTER
SEVENTEEN

Paris had chosen to go down to the first floor and escort Sydney Salinas up to their eighth floor offices. After he signed in at the security desk that was located within the building's lobby, she led him to a bank of elevators where she extended her hand and pressed the UP button, which was located on a brass panel affixed to the wall.

Paris couldn't help but notice how handsome this Sydney guy was. Her sister had obviously failed to mention to her that their soon-to-be suitor was so young. She didn't know why, but for some reason she was expecting Mr. Salinas to be a much older gentleman, maybe in his sixties or so. He appeared to be dressed comfortably, sporting a pair of blue jeans, white button-down shirt, black pinstriped designer suit jacket and a pair of black designer dress shoes.

"What a fine office building you have here," he commented, running his hand through his jet-black hair.

"Thank you. We just relocated here recently," she replied.

The elevator doors separated and he stood to one side, allowing Paris to enter first. She thanked him again. He flashed a broad smile, displaying his straight white teeth, which looked like a small picket fence encircling his mouth.

"Where did you relocate from?" he asked.

"The downtown area."

"I see. And you like this location better?"

"We absolutely love it!" Paris beamed.

He flashed his smile again.

There was a certain boyish-charm about him, Paris thought to herself, admiring his complexion, which was a café au lait hue.

They continued to exchange small talk in the elevator as they ascended to the eighth floor.

Milan sat quietly in Paris' office awaiting the return of her sister and Sydney Salinas. It was decided that they would meet in Paris' office because she had a small round conference table in a corner of her office, which seated four. And the main conference room, which seated twelve at the table, would have been overwhelming for just the three of them.

"You must be Milan!" Sydney greeted her as Paris led him into the office. She closed the door behind them.

Milan stood from her chair as Sydney approached. They shook hands firmly. "It's so nice to meet you, Mr. Salinas," Milan returned his greeting.

He was carrying a black leather GUCCI attaché case, which he leaned against the wall.

"Please, have a seat," Milan told him.

He seated himself between the two sisters.

"I must say that it is indeed a pleasure to meet the both of you," he said.

"Likewise, Mr. Salinas," Milan said. Paris nodded her head in agreement to the same.

"Ladies, I must insist that we be on a first name basis, if that's all right with you?"

"Of course," Paris answered.

"Good. After all, based on my research, I do believe that you two are just a bit my senior," he spoke jokingly.

"Well, I guess we shouldn't be surprised that you already know so much about us," Milan said.

Paris added, "Considering your interest in acquiring our agency."

"Yes, I've done my homework. However, I must say that the photographs that I've seen of you two in the media were highly understated. Your beauty in person is astonishing!"

The twins blushed. "So far you're doing a great job of buttering us up," Milan stated.

"I must speak the truth," he said, careful to make steady but warm eye contact with both of them. "Oh, before I forget," he began as he reached inside the breast pocket of his jacket and retrieved two of his business cards and handed one to each sister. "All of my numbers are on there," he told them. "So I'm always accessible."

"What would we do without the technological wonders of communications these days?" Milan remarked.

"Most of us couldn't survive," Sydney replied.

"Well, I regret having given my son's school the number to my office," Paris stated. Prior to Sydney's arrival, she'd been engaged in another annoying conversation with Tristan's first-grade teacher.

"Yes, I remember reading that one of you had a child," he said.

"That *one* would be me," Paris confirmed, holding up her hand.

"Well, I'm sure you are as successful as a mother as you have been with your agency," he told her.

"That's a sweet thing to say, Sydney. Thank you."

"Well, I take my hat off to you, Paris. I mean my mother raised me as a single parent. My father died from a brain tumor when I was only four."

"We're sorry to hear that," Milan spoke.

"Thanks."

"Your mother heads the ad agency, right?" Paris asked.

"Yes. She, too, was sort of thrust into the business after my father died. You see it had been his agency. My mother had never worked in advertising, least of all an ad agency."

"What's her background?" Milan was curious.

"She'd been a fashion model throughout her late teens and early twenties. She got pregnant with me when she was twenty-eight, but didn't actually marry my father until I was age three. And then, one year later, he died. My mother was thirty-two at the time. My father had been ten years older than she."

"How old is your mother now? If you don't mind me asking?" Paris wanted to know.

"She's fifty-three now. Still as beautiful as ever."

While Sydney had no trace of an accent, Paris was curious

about his ethnicity. "Sydney, forgive me for asking this, but is your ethnicity *Latino*?"

He smiled. "I was born in Miami, so I guess that makes me an American. However, both my parents came from Mexico."

"Well, you didn't seem to have an accent, which is why I was curious," Paris said.

"I know. People tell me that I have the *look*, but not the voice."

The three of them shared laughs.

"You grew up without a dad, and we grew up without a mother," Milan spoke solemnly.

He shook his head. "Yes, I'd also read about that unfortunate predicament. I take it you've never heard from her?"

"Not a single word," uttered Paris. "And we're at a point in our lives now where we no longer think about her."

Milan added, "That's true. In fact, we have an Aunt who's been more like a mother to us all of our lives."

"Well, it's good that you had someone else."

"We were blessed in that regard. As a matter of fact, she also works here at the agency," Paris stated.

"Really?"

"In our HR department. She oversees *health and benefits*."

"Well, I'm sure she must be very proud of you both. You've done an incredible job taking over this agency," he complimented them.

Sydney then began to provide them with details about SALINAS WORLDWIDE. He gave them a rundown of their key clients. He explained to them their interest in possibly acquiring the ALEXANDER AGENCY was due in large part to his mother. He shared with them her request for him to begin monitoring their agency a little over a year ago. Their interest also had to do with SALINAS WORLDWIDE'S quest to become a complete *multicultural* advertising agency. Not only do they want to specialize in marketing to Latinos, but also to African-Americans and Asians as well.

Although the twins' ad agency had just lost a significant client, Sydney told them that his mother's interest in acquiring them remained high. She believed that the ALEXANDER AGENCY had a very impressive track record and she was also impressed with the litany of creative awards that they'd received over the years. Several ADDY and CLIO awards had been bestowed upon their agency under their father's leadership. But over the past year, the twins' had also garnered a few impressive accolades.

Milan and Paris took turns providing Sydney with information about their agency. Although, he'd already put together quite an informative portfolio on his own. He asked them if he could spend a couple of days just hanging around the offices. He wanted to try and get a feel for the atmosphere as well as the people. The twins agreed that his presence would be welcomed.

"Where are you staying?" Paris asked.

"I was fortunate enough to get a room right across the street from you guys – at the WESTIN."

"Oh, that's a lovely hotel," Milan remarked.

"Well, I've had the privilege of staying at WESTIN HOTELS whenever I visit our Los Angeles and New York offices," Sydney shared.

The twins gave him a tour of their offices and introduced him to all three department heads for account management, creative and media. They also wanted him to meet Aunt Millie, but unfortunately she had a doctor's appointment and was not in the office. They assured him that he'd have an opportunity to meet her before his trip ended.

"Can I interest you two ladies in joining me for dinner this evening?" Sydney posed the question, as they returned to Paris' office.

The twins exchanged demure glances at one another.

"Well . . . unfortunately I have to meet with my builder this evening," Milan stated.

"Building a new home?"

"Reluctantly, yes," she answered. "My sister talked me into it."

"Hey, it's a very nice development," Paris defended herself. "Besides, we can stay close to one another."

"Oh, so you live there already?" Sydney asked Paris.

"Not yet. My home won't be ready for another three months. And Milan is just starting to build, so she's got about eight to ten months."

"Atlanta sounds a lot like the Dallas area," Sydney said. "There's still a lot of home building going on there too."

"Actually, this development has been up a while, but new home sites are still available,"

"I guess I was sold on the golf course," Milan interjected.

Sydney's eyebrows arched. "Golf? Do you play?"

"We both have had lessons," Milan answered.

"Yeah, but I'm not sure if it has helped our playing ability," Paris laughed. "But our dad was a big fan of golf and he wanted us to at least *learn* about the game."

"Well, I must say that you ladies have impressed me considerably."

"What about you, Sydney? Are you a golfer?" Paris asked him.

He nodded modestly. "I try and play as often as I can. But of course, the weather has been crazy in Dallas this winter so I haven't had many opportunities to get out."

"Same here," Paris replied.

"So, what are *your* plans for this evening?" he asked Paris, the one he found himself more drawn to.

"Actually, I'm free."

He beamed at her. "I'll take that as a yes for dinner this evening."

Paris gave him a knowing smile. "Dinner it is."

Sydney needed to make a few business calls. Paris led him to a small vacant office down the hall. "Feel free to make yourself comfortable," she told him. "Take all the time you need."

He thanked her.

When Paris returned to her office, Milan was sitting on the sofa with her legs crossed. "I thought you were supposed to meet with Scotty this evening?" Milan reminded her sister, playfully.

"Scotty *who*?"

They both erupted into laughter.

CHAPTER
EIGHTEEN

Mirabella Salinas had become angry with her son as she spoke with him on the telephone. She'd given him an assignment that should have taken no more than one day to complete. He hadn't been sent to Atlanta to *close* a deal with them on his first visit. She clearly explained to her protégé that the meeting was strictly for exploratory reasons.

At six-foot-one, Mirabella was a towering figure of ageless beauty. Although she was fifty-three years of age, the former fashion model could have very easily passed for a mere thirty-five.

Twenty-five floors above downtown Dallas, she stood in her posh office gazing at the skyline while she held the cordless phone to her ear. The more she listened to her son attempt to explain why he was remaining in Atlanta for a few more days, the more disconcerted she was becoming.

"Mother, I realize that I was supposed to come back home on Wednesday. But I'm going to stay a couple more days and I'll fly out on Sunday morning," Sydney explained.

"¿Por qué, Sydney? ¿Por qué?" Mirabella said in her thick Spanish accent, asking him *why, why*?

Sydney hated it when she spoke in Spanish to him. One reason was because he spoke and understood very little Spanish himself and also whenever his mother did so it usually meant that she was angry.

"It's only *two* more days, mother."

"Sydney, three days already you've been there!" she reminded him, switching back to English.

"And I'll be here two more days."

Mirabella exhaled deeply. "What have you accomplished so far, son?"

"A lot."

"Like what?"

"Well, I've had some in-depth conversations with both Paris and Milan. I've also had the opportunity to just hang around the office and observe everyone at work. And mother, I must say that these employees have such an incredible amount of support for one another."

"What are their feelings about the acquisition?"

"Well, they are certainly willing to consider a proposal from us."

"You didn't get into any specifics, did you Sydney?"

"No, mother. Of course not."

"Good. We will need to see a statement of their financial position. Are they aware of this?"

"Yes, mother. They're very intelligent young women."

"I'm not surprised," she said, speaking softly to herself.

"What's that, mother?"

"Nothing. As long as they understand our need for due diligence to be performed."

"Trust me. They know the process."

Mirabella returned to her oversized desk and sat in the overstuffed high-back chair. "Sydney, it's Friday. I understand if you must stay today. But why not leave this evening? What is there to do tomorrow? A Saturday?"

He hesitated. He didn't want to venture down this road because his mother could sometimes be over-protective of him where women were involved. "If you must know, I plan to have dinner again with Paris this evening and then play a round of golf with her and Milan as well as another gentleman on Saturday."

Silence filled the distance between them.

"Mother? Are you there?"

Mirabella swallowed the lump in her throat. "Again?"

"What?"

"You said 'dinner again with Paris', Sydney."

"Well, that's because I had dinner with her on Tuesday. Mother, Paris is such a sweet woman. Actually, they both are. But there's something about Paris that intrigues me."

"Sydney," Mirabella began softly. "I understand that you are a handsome hombre, and that you are in the presence of two very beautiful senioritas. But you must remain focused. This is a business trip. I do not want you to do anything that will compromise your judgment."

"I'm not planning to, mother."

"Then I think you should reconsider this *dinner* thing."

Sydney chuckled. "Mother, you worry too much about me. I'm twenty-five years old. You've raised an incredible son and you've taught me well. Believe in that, all right?"

"Sí," she answered. "Your ticket? Have you changed your plane ticket?"

"I've already spoken with the airline and there shouldn't be a problem changing my ticket. A small fee of course."

"You should have taken the corporate jet," she lightly reprimanded him.

"Mother, you know how I hate to fly. I'm certainly not crazy about those little planes."

"*Little*? Many young executives would love to fly on business in a GULFSTREAM IV. When you are a busy executive, Sydney, *speed*, *comfort* and *convenience* become very important."

"True, mother. But when the *busy executive* is afraid of heights, *calm nerves* become more important."

"Fear is all in your head, son. It is within your heart where you are brave. ¿Comprendo?" (understand?)

Sydney smiled. "Lo comprendo perfectamente," he replied, telling his mother that he understood perfectly.

CHAPTER
NINETEEN

ALICIA Keys had just finished singing *If I Ain't Got You*, one of Paris' favorite tracks from her latest CD, when she turned her desert-platinum colored INFINITI G35 COUPE into the driveway of her townhouse. Earlier she had dropped off Sydney at his hotel. Admittedly, she was thrilled to learn that he'd extended his trip a few days. He'd also invited her, along with Milan and Blade, to play a round of golf tomorrow. Although it was January, the forecast was calling for temperatures to be near sixty.

Paris was about to press the button on the garage door opener, which was affixed to her visor, when a car pulled directly behind her. For a moment she froze. The headlights were bright as she peered through her rearview mirror. She couldn't tell how many people were in the car nor could she make out the type of car it was. Quickly, she checked her car doors to make certain that they were locked. Then she reached inside her purse, which was setting on the passenger seat, and retrieved the pepper spray, holding it firmly in her hand.

The door to the driver's side on the car behind her opened. Her heart was racing. She wondered if she should be dialing *nine-one-one* on her cell phone at this particular moment. Who the heck was this?

The tall bulky figure emerged from the vehicle.

It was Scotty Sims.

When she caught a glimpse of him through her side view mirror swaggering up her driveway like he owned the place, her fear quickly turned into anger.

"What is your problem!" she shouted, jumping from her car.

Scotty threw both hands up. "Whoa, now. No need to go ballistic on a brother!"

Paris wanted to slap him right across his no-good face. She could see that his eyes were bloodshot and the liquor on his breath intoxicated the nighttime air. But she restrained herself. "Don't you ever do that to me again!"

"Do what? I, I just got here. I ain't do nothing to you!" His speech was slurred.

"You know what I'm talking about, Scotty! I don't want to find you parked outside my house waiting for me to come home. Who do you think you are?"

"Hey, I wouldn't even be here if you hadn't dissed me."

"Dis you how?"

"Oh, so now you tryin' to play me for a fool, too? I know you been hangin' out with that Latino dude. Is that why you canceled on me Tuesday?"

"Listen to me, Scotty," Paris began, wagging her index finger in his face like she was *Alicia Calaway* from SURVIVOR. "Who I choose to hang out with is none of your business. And the very next time you decide that you want to pull up behind my car with your lights shining all bright, you better hope that I don't have more than pepper spray inside my purse."

He flashed her a crooked smile. She was taken aback by how much he'd changed. He was twenty-six just like her, yet he looked twice his age. Drugs and excessive alcohol use had a way of making over one's appearance.

"What you gon do?" he let out a drunken laugh. "I know you ain't gon shoot me 'cause I'm yo baby's daddy!"

"Humph. Don't tell me what I will or will not do, Scotty Sims. You don't know me well enough to be speculating like that."

He reached his arms out towards her. Paris took a couple of steps backwards. Stumbling over his own feet he fell to the ground. "Ouch! Why you wanna push me down?"

"I didn't push you, Scotty. You're *drunk*!"

Slowly, he rose to his feet, wobbling a few seconds before finally steadying himself against her car. "You got a phat ride, Paris," he said, blinking his eyes in an attempt to focus on the car more clearly. "I ain't know you was balling like that."

"There's a lot about me you know nothing about," she said, standing with her arms crossed. "You still haven't said why you're here? At eleven o'clock at night?"

His head dropped suddenly, like it was too heavy for him to hold up. He raised it up again and tried to stare into her eyes. "You looking fly, Paris. Real fly!"

She was about ready to tell him to get his sorry behind into his car and leave. But it was obvious that he was in no condition to drive anywhere. And she knew in all good conscience that she couldn't send him away like this. He was a D-U-I disaster just waiting to happen.

Scotty looked up at the townhouse. "Paris, I need to crash at your crib."

"That's not going to happen, Scotty."

He wobbled some more, head dangling like it was about to fall off his body altogether. "Don't trip on me, now. You and me . . . back in the day . . . we had mad love for each other."

"Don't even go there, Scotty. What you and I had together was a very long time ago."

"I miss kickin' it with my girl," he mumbled.

Paris glanced at her watch. She was certain that both Nikki and Tristan were asleep. She decided that she was going to drop Scotty off at a motel. He could come and pick up his car in the morning.

"Come on, let's go," she told him, grabbing him by the arm and leading him around her car to the passenger side.

"Hey, what you doin'?"

"I'm taking you to a motel."

He grinned triumphantly. "Gettin' tired of the lil' Mexican dude already? I guess you know who's da bomb!"

"Don't flatter yourself, Scotty," she told him as she eased him into the car and strapped the seatbelt on him. "You'll be sleeping there by yourself."

Before he could respond, she quickly slammed the door. He continued to talk as if she was standing there listening to him.

Paris walked over to Scotty's car. The engine was still running. Her garage was a single-car garage so she'd have to park his car on the street. She got an eerie feeling as she got behind the wheel of the Lexus. The exterior was black but the interior was a cream color, just like it had been in her father's car. She noticed several empty liquor bottles strewn across the floor on the passenger's side. Why would he even consider driving drunk and risk the possibility of taking someone's life? Not to mention his own.

She could see his head bobbing around in the front seat of her car. She needed to hurry up and get this fool to a motel. As the gear was slid into reverse, Paris backed out of the driveway and parked the car on the street. She shut off the engine and got out of the car and then locked the doors. As she moved away from the car, that eerie feeling enveloped her again. Of course, every time she saw a Lexus LS model on the road, it conjured up memories of her father and how much he had loved his car.

Paris got into her car and strapped herself in. She glanced over at Scotty. His head was leaning against the window. He was fast asleep.

For a brief moment she allowed herself to feel sorry for him. But then the question struck her like a lightning bolt – how could this man, with no job, and not even his own place to live, afford to be driving around in a LEXUS LS430? When she'd gotten into his car, she saw his wallet lying on the passenger seat. Reluctantly, she peeked inside. There wasn't a single dollar bill. But there were three condom packs inside one of the compartments. She had decided not to leave the wallet in the car.

Paris could only shake her head as she took another glance over at him – Tristan's father. He'd been a star quarterback throughout high school with an even more promising football future at the college level. Yet, one injury had derailed it all. He'd said that it was the *injury* that led him to abuse alcohol and drugs. She told him that he was simply making excuses for himself. One thing she did know for certain, he was not abusing drugs and alcohol when he'd told her that he *cared* for her. That she was the *only* girl that he wanted to be with. That he wanted to spend the *rest* of his life with her. That he couldn't imagine anyone else being the mother of his children.

It had been *Scotty Michael Sims* who told her all those things. The person with whom she had shared the same thoughts and emotions. Of course she had believed every word from his mouth.

Why was she now feeling sorry for him? It was he who turned his back on her and their son. She had given him no reason whatsoever to treat her the way he did. Once she told him that she was pregnant, he made the decision to basically have nothing to do with her. And he never told her why.

No. She would not make his troubles her troubles. This was his cross to bear. His burden to carry.

People make choices every day. Some good. Some bad. Some indifferent.

Paris found a LA QUINTA INN over by the mall. She wasn't all that crazy about him being in Alpharetta so close to her home. She'd considered driving him to midtown or some place. But it was late and she didn't want to have to drive any longer than necessary.

She left him asleep in the car while she went inside and rented a room. She made it clear to the desk clerk that she was renting the room for someone else and that it was for one night only. The desk clerk affected a smile. She figured that he didn't believe her, but at the moment she cared very little about that.

The room was located downstairs on the other side of the building. She pulled her car into the parking space and hurried to the passenger side and began to awake Scotty by shaking him. He moaned and grunted a few times as he got out of the car. The stench of liquor on him was almost unbearable. Her car would definitely need detailing after tonight.

Once inside the room she allowed his body to flop across the bed. She had no intentions of trying to make him comfortable. Neither his shoes were removed nor any other article of clothing.

Paris walked over to the desk in the room and opened the center drawer. Taking the blank sheet of letterhead from the drawer she jotted down a note telling him to come and pick up his car when he awoke. She placed the note on the nightstand and set his car keys on top of it. Then she fished his wallet from her purse and placed it next to the note as well before she made her way towards the door.

Paris stopped just before leaving the room. She looked over her shoulder at Scotty. He was sprawled faced down on the bed breathing heavily. She closed her eyes at that moment and prayed silently for him.

She walked back over to the nightstand and picked up his wallet. In the note she'd told him to call himself a cab to get to her house, but she realized that there was no money in his wallet. She reached inside her purse and pulled out her own wallet and retrieved a one hundred dollar bill and stuck it inside his. "You don't deserve anything that I've done for you tonight, Scotty Sims," she whispered. "But I haven't done it because of who you are, but because of who I am."

Darkness pervaded the room as she flipped the light switch. She closed the door to the room and hurried to her car. It was almost midnight. As she drove away from the Inn she fought back tears. She wasn't sure if she was crying for him or for herself. The tears quickly became sobs.

What had gone so terribly wrong between them? Why was he choosing to throw his life away? Could he not see the dangerous wrong that he was travelling on?

She dried her eyes with the back of her hand. It was too quiet around her so she reached over and turned on her CD player. Alicia Keys was still in there. Paris skipped to track number nine. The lyrics began to ooze from her speakers . . .

> You used to be my closest ally
> In this cold, cold world of deception and lies
> . . . Where did we go wrong, baby
> Did this cold, cold world turn us into stone . . .

More tears flowed as Paris internalized the lyrics. She couldn't believe how emotional she'd become. The tears had blurred her eyes to the point where she had to pull her car over to the side of the road. Gripping the steering wheel with both hands she allowed her head to drop against the steering wheel. As Alicia Keys continued to sing, *'when we're gonna wake up . . . before it's too late'*, Paris cried even harder.

She realized that this was a necessary cleansing. Scotty Sims would never be a part of her life again.

Paris lifted her head as she heard the sound of rain pelting her windshield. In that moment she thought back to when she was a little girl. She remembered telling Milan one day that whenever it rained it must have meant that God was crying up in Heaven. Milan had simply laughed at her notion and told her that God didn't ever have to cry about anything – He had everything.

To this day, Paris wasn't so sure about her sister's reasoning. God loves everyone. But not everyone loves God. That had to be enough to make Him cry at times.

She dried her eyes again, turned on the wipers and headed home. As she drove she thought to herself, perhaps God cried for people who could no longer cry for themselves.

Maybe, just maybe, this sudden downpour of rain was simply God crying for Scotty Sims because Scotty's life was so messed up right now.

Or, maybe God was worried about her getting mixed up with Scotty again. Maybe He was trying to remind her of all the hurt Scotty had caused her.

Maybe all of this rain wasn't tears of unhappiness from Heaven. Maybe they were tears of joy. Maybe God was so happy that she would not allow Scotty to affect her life anymore that He cried tears of joy tonight.

Yeah, just maybe.

CHAPTER
TWENTY

Rain continued to attack the Atlanta area on Saturday morning. For some it was great weather for sleeping in. Sydney had gotten up around seven A.M. and peeked out his hotel window. It was obvious that they would not be honoring their nine o'clock tee time. He phoned Paris and told her that they'd have to take a rain check on golf. Although still somewhat asleep, Paris had mumbled that it was okay and that she would call Milan and then have Milan call Blade.

Sydney retreated back to his bed and shielded himself beneath the covers. He closed his eyes and listened as the raindrops beat against the window. In no time at all he'd drifted away to sleep again.

An hour later Paris awoke to the sound of her telephone ringing. "Hello," she said, her voice groggy.

"Good morning, Sis. It's me."

"Hey, Milan."

"Are you still in the bed?"

"Mmm Mmm."

"I guess you and Sydney hung out pretty late last night, huh?"

Paris sat up in bed. She attempted to clear the cobwebs from her head by shaking it. "Actually, Sydney and I didn't stay out that long. We finished dinner around ten and then I dropped him off at the hotel. I guess we figured that we'd be getting up early for golf this morning."

"Speaking of golf, I assume we're not playing this morning?" Milan said, remembering why she'd called her sister in the first place.

"Yeah, it's off. Sydney called this morning and said he'd cancel the tee time. You'll need to call Blade."

"I just got off the phone with him before I called you. He was actually calling to cancel. Said he woke up this morning with a throbbing headache. I told him that I was pretty sure that none of us would be playing this morning."

"Yeah. I was kinda looking forward to getting out there today. I haven't played in a while."

"Yes, so was I. But hey, spring is just around the corner."

Paris stretched the phone cord across her bed far enough so that she could glance out the window. The black Lexus was still parked in front of her house. "You'll never believe what happened last night, girl?"

"Just tell me."

"Scotty was parked outside my house when I got home."

"Scotty! What was his problem now?"

"First, he nearly scared the daylights out of me . . ."

"Oh my god, what did he do?" Milan interrupted.

"Well, when I pulled into the driveway he pulled in right behind me. But I didn't know it was him. So I got scared. I mean I didn't know if some fool was about to rob me, jack my car or what!"

"What did you do?"

"At first nothing. I just sat there too scared to move. I mean I thought about opening the garage but then I figured that if this was some fool, I didn't want him getting into the house also. So, I grabbed my pepper spray and just waited. Then Scotty staggers his drunk behind from the car."

"What was he even doing at your house late at night?"

"Apparently he'd been sitting out there just waiting for me to come home. Then he starts trippin' about Sydney."

"Sydney? How does he know anything about Sydney?"

"I have no idea. I'm assuming he's been following me."

"Listen Paris, you need to get a restraining order against him," Milan spoke firmly.

"Milan, I'm not worried about Scotty doing anything to me. Especially not last night. He could barely stand up straight."

Milan sighed. "It makes you wonder if his sorry behind even made it home safely last night if he was as drunk as you say," she remarked.

Paris went on to tell her sister about her decision to drive Scotty to a motel and leave his car parked at her house. Milan came close to scolding her sister for doing *anything* for Scotty. She told Paris that he was simply trying to worm his way back into her life.

While they continued their conversation, Tristan came into his mom's room. "Hi, mommy!" he greeted, diving onto her bed.

"Shh," Paris said, placing her finger to her lips. "Mommy's on the phone with Auntie Milan."

Tristan started grabbing at the phone. "Let me talk to Auntie Milan! Please, mommy! Can I talk on the phone?"

Paris tried to scoot him off the bed, but to no avail. "Hey, your nephew wants to talk to you," she told Milan as she handed Tristan the phone.

"Hi, Auntie Milan!" Tristan shouted into the phone.

"Hey there, little man! Did you sleep good last night?"

"Uh huh."

"Auntie misses you!"

"Can you come over my house and play with me?"

"Of course I'll come over and play with my favorite nephew!"

"Yea!" Tristan screamed. He dropped the phone onto the bed and started jumping up and down on the bed.

"Tristan, stop that before you fall and bust your head wide open!" Paris told him.

"I'm tough, mommy!" he replied and continued to bounce like he was on a trampoline.

"Hey, girl," Paris said, putting the phone to her ear again. "Your nephew is going to hurt himself by jumping up and down on my bed like a little monkey."

Milan laughed. "I heard him say that he was *tough*."

"Yeah, that's his favorite word lately. But we'll see how tough he is when he cracks that big head of his."

"Don't you be talking about my nephew's head," Milan shot back. "He just takes after his mother!"

"Well, if you're trying to call me a big head, then you might "as well call yourself one," Paris said, chuckling.

Tristan finally hopped down from the bed and sprinted over to the window to look at the rain coming down. When he peeked through the blinds he saw the car parked outside. "Mommy! Mister Scotty's outside! I see his Lexus!"

"No, sweetheart. Mister Scotty isn't outside, he just had to leave his car here last night," Paris explained.

"Can I go play in it again? Please mommy!"

"Tristan, no. Now mommy's trying to talk on the telephone, okay?"

"What's he so excited about?" Milan asked.

"He just looked out the window and saw Scotty's car parked outside," answered Paris. "And now he wants to know if he can go out and play in it."

"Why would he ask that?"

"Well, right before Christmas Scotty had come by the house to drop off some gifts and Tristan had begged him to let him sit in his car."

"And you let him?"

"No! I wasn't even at home at the time. But apparently Nikki allowed him to – against my wishes of course."

"He must have a pretty cool car if Tristan got all excited about it."

"He does. And how he can afford to drive a big Lexus, I'll never know."

"A Lexus!"

"That's right. The LS430 model. A black one."

"I'm sure it's not his," Milan stated. "Probably some female's car."

"Yeah, probably."

Tristan made a beeline back to the bed. "Mommy, did grandpa tell Mister Scotty he was a good speller when he wrote grandpa's name on his car too?"

Paris wasn't paying her son any attention at the moment. "Tristan, I told you that I'm trying to talk on the phone!" she said, her voice much firmer.

"Wait, Paris! What did Tristan say about his grandpa and Scotty?"

"What?" Paris had tuned Tristan out.

"Just then. I thought I heard him asking something about

"grandpa telling Scotty that he was a good speller?"

Paris thought for second or two. That was exactly what her son had just said. "Hold on a minute, Milan." Tristan had wandered off the bed and was now sifting through items on his mother's dresser. "Tristan, come here please." He trotted back over to the bed. "Did you say something about grandpa and Mister Scotty?"

"Uh huh."

"Well, mommy didn't hear you. What is it you wanted to know?"

"I was asking you if grandpa told Mister Scotty that he was a good speller too?" Tristan repeated.

"Sweetheart, why would you ask that?"

"Because."

"Because what?"

"Remember that time when Mister Scotty let me play in his car?"

"Yeah. Mommy was at work but I remember Nikki telling me about it."

"I told Nikki mommy because you wouldn't let me tell you. Nikki said that you was very busy."

Paris quickly recalled that conversation. Her son had been trying to tell her something and she vividly remembers hurrying him off the phone. "Yeah, well mommy's sorry for not listening to you. So tell me now what it was you wanted me to know."

Tristan plopped down on the bed next to his mom. "I was going to tell you that Mister Scotty has grandpa's name on the back of the car seat just like grandpa had in his Lexus!"

Paris' face became a mask of horror.

"Oh my god, Paris," was all Milan could say on the other end. Both their minds were racing with the unthinkable.

"Want me to show you, mommy? I can show you in the car outside!"

Trying to stay composed, Paris said "Milan, get over here right away!"

"I'm on my way," her sister answered.

Paris hung up the phone. She could hear her pulse roaring in her ears. "Dear God, please let this be some weird coincidence."

CHAPTER
TWENTY-ONE

There were only two exits to travel between her Roswell condominium and her sister's Alpharetta townhouse. Milan had hurriedly thrown on a pair of sweat pants and shirt when she got off the phone with Paris. Her hair was looking crazy when she glanced in the bathroom's mirror, but there was no time to do it justice so she grabbed her COACH bucket hat from the closet and slapped it on her head.

As twin sisters they often bought the same style of clothes. Their automobile purchases were no different. While the color of Paris' INFINITI G35 COUPE was *desert platinum*, Milan's was a *Caribbean blue*.

Oblivious to the falling rain, which made for slick pavements, Milan sped up GEORGIA 400 with a million thoughts racing through her head. Was it really possible that Scotty Sims had something to do with their father's death? Although, Paris did tell her that he said that he'd been back in the area for some three years. And he'd gotten himself mixed up with drugs and alcohol.

Milan began to shake her head. "No, no," she whispered to herself. "Not even *he* could be that low down." Yet, Tristan had said that his grandpa's name was on the back of Scotty's car seat. How could that be? And for Tristan to recognize something like that it had to be true. She remembered how proud he was when he'd written his grandpa's name on the back of the headrest. And her father had been just as proud of Tristan when he found the scribbling. Her father thought that what his grandson had done was cute. Of course, Tristan's grandpa had already spoiled him rotten.

The cell phone rang.

"Hello."

"Milan, where are you?" Paris asked, her voice cracking.

"I'm coming up on your exit now."

"Good. I called Aunt Millie. She's on her way as well."

"That was a good idea. Have you gone out to the car to look?"

"No. I'm too nervous. Besides, I don't have the keys."

"Well, you should be able to look through the window and see."

"Yeah, I know. But I'm going to wait for you."

"All right," Milan said before ending the call. She decided to also phone Blade. If this turns out to be the worst-case scenario then they might need his legal expertise. If nothing else, she knew that she would need his support.

CHAPTER
TWENTY-TWO

Mildred Alexander had already been up and about when her niece called her. She'd never been much of a late sleeper herself. In fact, if she slept past six-thirty in the morning she considered that *late*.

Growing up with Everson, who had been only two years older, he'd often use her as his alarm clock. She woke him up for school. She woke him up each morning when he'd gotten his first paper route at the age of fourteen. And she woke him up for any other time-sensitive matter that he faced.

She had been very close to her brother. He'd always looked out for her and she'd always looked out for him. She remembered the very morning that Everson had called her and told her that Nicole was missing. She knew how much her brother loved his wife. She would eventually pray with him on many nights for her safe return. But she could tell that the more time passed, the more his hope faded.

Mildred had no idea what would cause her brother's wife to just walk away. And while she hadn't spent a lot of time with Nicole, the two of them got along good. Nicole was four years younger than her brother, but she knew that such a minor difference in age really had no effect on their relationship.

It was, however, apparent to her that Nicole did not want children right away. She and Everson had only been married for a couple of years when she found out that she was pregnant with the twins. But, Mildred always thought that both her brother and his wife were thrilled about the pregnancy. Nicole hadn't been working at the time, she was in between jobs, and so it seemed like an excellent time for her to have a baby.

If there had been a negative to their marriage, it would have probably been the fact that Everson traveled a lot. He worked as a management consultant and the job often required him to leave home on a Sunday night and not return until Friday evening.

Mildred was certain, however, that her brother's traveling schedule did not cause his wife to abandon him. She suspected that the woman wasn't altogether *there* mentally. A woman just didn't wake up one morning and decide to abandon her infant twins – beautiful girls.

She didn't hesitate to step in and assist her brother in raising the twins. She absolutely adored them. Helping to care for Milan and Paris actually had filled a deep void in her own life. It had never been a matter of her not wanting children, or even a marriage, but a cheating fiancé was about as close to marriage that she came, and it would be as close that she would ever allow herself to get.

Mildred was so proud of Everson when she learned that he was going to resign his job as a management consultant so that he could spend more time with his daughters. He did not want them being raised in a daycare facility where he didn't believe that they would get the personal attention small children should have and deserve. And Mildred couldn't care for them on a full-time basis because at that time she worked full-time as a human resources consultant with a major insurance company. But she certainly would go over to her brother's house in the evenings and help the twins with their homework, take them to school events and basically, just give her brother a break. Even though Everson had set up an office in his home after he'd resigned from the consulting firm, she knew that he still could use a break now and then.

As she made the turn onto the road that led to Paris' townhouse, she wondered what was so urgent that would make her niece insist that she come over right away. Paris did not want to get into it over the telephone and Mildred decided not to press her on it.

When she arrived at Paris' house she saw Milan's car parked in the driveway. The driveway could only fit one car so she'd have to park on the street. She drove down to the cul-de-sac and turned around. There was another car parked in front of her niece's house, which she didn't recognize. She decided to park her car directly behind the black Lexus. Aside from the exterior color and those gaudy rims on the car, Mildred thought it resembled her brother's car. Of course, his Lexus was never found after it had been carjacked by two thugs on that awful summer's night.

Mildred popped the umbrella as she stepped from her car. The rain was beginning to slow somewhat but it was still coming down hard enough for her to use an umbrella. She hurried up the walkway to the front door. Before she could press the doorbell, the door swung open.

"Hey, Aunt Millie," Paris greeted her. "We've been waiting for you. Come on in."

CHAPTER
TWENTY-THREE

Nikki had taken Tristan with her to the mall. Paris told her that she had an important meeting with Milan and Aunt Millie and that she didn't want Tristan disrupting them. Nikki was delighted to spend Saturday morning at the mall, even if it meant bringing Tristan along. And considering the fact that Paris had also given her two hundred dollars in cash might have attributed to her enthusiasm.

The three of them were sitting in the living room. Paris sat in a chair opposite the sofa where Milan and Aunt Millie were seated. Paris had brought Aunt Millie up to speed on what was happening.

"When I drove up and saw that Lexus parked out there, the first thing that went through my mind was that it sure did look like Everson's car," Aunt Millie said.

"Well, there's only way to find out for certain," Milan stated, referring to the fact that they would have to go out and look inside the car to see if it did have Tristan's scribbling on the back of the headrest.

"Let me grab my jacket," Paris told them. She went to the closet in the foyer and retrieved her leather jacket. The rain had subsided so both Milan and Aunt Millie left their umbrellas inside.

Holding hands, the three women walked slowly down the walkway towards the car. They stopped just a few feet from the car. The windows were tinted, which made it difficult for them to see inside. Aunt Millie walked over and pressed her face to the glass on the rear driver's side window. She squinted until her eyes were nearly closed but she was not able to clearly see the back of the headrest.

Milan walked around to the other side of the car and attempted to look inside from that angle. She couldn't see anything either.

"I'm so tempted to just take something and bust this window out," Paris said, her nerves starting to get the best of her.

Feeling helpless, they stood and stared at the car.

"What I don't understand is," began Milan. "If this is daddy's car and Scotty had something to do with carjacking it and killing him, why would he go through the trouble to paint the outside of the car, tint the windows and put these ghetto-looking rims on it and not clean off the scribbling?"

"Because he's stupid!" Paris shouted. "Plus, he's so high on drugs and alcohol these days that he probably hasn't even seen the writing!"

Aunt Millie shook her head. "It's been a year and a half now. You'd think the boy would have seen it by now."

Milan braced herself onto the car's trunk and tried to peer through the back window. It was still too dark. "Why the heck did he darken these windows so much for?" she said in frustration as she hopped off the trunk.

"Who knows," Aunt Millie answered. "You see a lot of these young people doing that to their cars. I guess they're trying to make their cars look like the ones in those music videos. I've seen them with chains hanging from rearview mirrors, wheels spinning around and music so loud you can hear it a mile away."

Blade's Range Rover turned onto the street.

"Here comes Blade," Milan said, spotting the SUV heading their way.

They watched as Blade beeped his horn as he drove past them down to the cul-de-sac where he turned around and parked behind Aunt Millie's Volvo.

"I got here as quickly as I could," he said, exiting the vehicle. He greeted Milan first, giving her a quick hug, then he spoke hello to Paris and Mildred. The difference in greetings did not go unnoticed as Paris and Aunt Millie shot cursory glances to one another.

"We've been trying to see inside the car," Milan told Blade. "But it's too dark."

Blade walked over to the car and gave a quick peek. "All of you believe that this is Everson's Lexus?"

"Well, obviously some changes have been made to the car. But the words *grandpa* scribbled on the back of that headrest will definitely confirm it," Paris answered.

After Milan had phoned Blade she also called Detective Hengess who'd been handling the case. He drove up in an unmarked police vehicle. The Detective introduced himself to each of them, although Aunt Millie had met with him during the early stages of the investigation. The twins had only spoken to him over the telephone.

"So y'all have reason to believe that this vehicle is the same one that your father was driving on the night in which he was murdered?"

His using the word *murdered* caught both sisters off guard. They both placed their hand over their mouths and fought back tears. The Detective immediately sensed that he might have spoken too bluntly. "Let me apologize to y'all. I don't mean to be insensitive to your tragedy."

Everyone nodded in acceptance of his apology.

"Do y'all know who owns this vehicle?" he asked.

Milan answered, "Well, like I told you over the phone, Detective Hengess, my sister's ex-boyfriend is driving this car now."

"Is that you Miss?" he asked, looking at Paris.

She nodded.

"And how long have you and your ex-boyfriend been broken up?"

"A very long time," Paris responded. "It's been over six years since we were together."

"I see. So, this ex-boyfriend . . ." the Detective paused. "By the way, what is his name?"

"Scotty," Paris answered. "Scotty Sims."

Detective Hengess retrieved a small notepad from the inside pocket of the khaki trench coat he was wearing. He jotted the name down. "Okay. Let's see here – as I was about "to say, this Scotty fella and you were no longer together well before the tragedy occurred?"

"That's correct," Paris answered.

"Well, now. Do we know if this Scotty fella was in town at the time of the incident?"

Milan and Paris exchanged dubious looks. Paris responded, "To be honest, Detective Hengess, at the time that I learned about my father's incident, Scotty Sims was the last person on my mind. So, in answer to your question, I have no idea where he was that night. But I do know that my son had written the words grandpa on the back headrest of my father's Lexus, and my son said he saw those same words on the back headrest of this Lexus," she pointed at the car. "Now, with all due respect, I think we should first look to see if my son was correct before we jump into all these questions."

"She's right, Detective," Blade spoke. "These questions might be a bit premature."

"I see y'alls point. I take it y'all don't have the keys to get inside the car?"

"Scotty has the keys," Paris told him.

He gave her a critical squint. "Y'all understand that I can't search this vehicle without a search warrant?"

The twins and Aunt Millie stared blankly at the Detective. "Give me a minute," he said before trotting over to his car.

"He's right," Blade spoke. "To obtain a search warrant he's got to demonstrate two things. First, he'll have to show probable cause that a specific crime has been committed. Second, he'll have to demonstrate probable cause that some type of physical evidence currently can be found in this vehicle."

"Oh, god," Milan said, emitting a frustrated sigh. "If Scotty knows we're on to him then he'll definitely clean up the car or try to get rid of it altogether."

As the Detective sat in his car talking on the phone, a white taxi pulled up to where they all were. Within seconds, the man of the hour emerged from the backseat.

"Wassup!" Scotty Sims grinned, looking like something the cat had dragged in.

CHAPTER
TWENTY-FOUR

Both of the twins along with Aunt Millie were poised to attack Scotty with a vengeance, but Blade quickly cautioned them to play it cool. He told them that they did not want to make him too suspicious.

Scotty walked over to them. He spoke non-verbally by giving one tilt of his head backwards. "Hey shorty, good looking out for a brother last night," he said to Paris. But Paris remained speechless.

Detective Hengess, though on the phone, watched as Scotty got out of the cab. And based on the chilly reception that the others had given him, the Detective assumed that the young man had to be the owner of the Lexus.

"Excuse me," the Detective said to Scotty, as he rejoined the group. "Are you Mister Sims?"

Scotty gave the Detective the once-over "Who's this dude?" he asked, although to no one in particular.

The Detective reached inside his trench coat and retrieved his badge. He held the shiny metal directly before the young man's eyes. "*Detective Hengess* from the Atlanta Police Department."

A troubled look spread across Scotty's face. "Police? I ain't do nothing!"

"I haven't accused you of anything, sir."

Paris piped in, "Uh, Scotty. The alarm in your car was set off earlier and we'd been trying to figure out how to turn it off "but we didn't have the keys." She knew that her father's car had an alarm system and she risked the assumption that all other Lexus cars had alarms as well. "The noise was so loud that we were . . ."

"And that's when the Detective drove by," Milan interrupted.

The Detective shot them both scorching glances. However, Scotty seemed to have bought into their stories because he quickly relaxed. "Yeah, it went off on me a couple times the other night," he said, fishing his keys from his pocket. "Let me just make sure ain't nobody been tryin' to mess with my ride," he chuckled, walking over to the driver's side door and inserting the key.

Everyone watched in anticipation. The twins held their breath, as if Scotty Sims was about to detonate a bomb.

The Detective saw no need to rush to anything. After all, he didn't have a search warrant so he decided to allow matters to unfold a moment.

Scotty climbed inside the car and began to inspect the vehicle, opening and closing the glove compartment, the ashtray, and he pulled down the visors. No one knew precisely what he was supposed to be looking for.

"I didn't know you owned a Lexus, Scotty?" Paris spoke.

He beamed with pride. "Yeah, it's a dope ride ain't it?"

Aunt Millie was giving Paris the *eye* trying to communicate to her to get inside the car, but Paris kept shaking her head 'no'.

"Tristan said that he got a chance to play in it one day," Paris said.

"Yeah, the lil' dude kept asking me if he could. I mean what could I say? The lil' dude's my son!"

All three women cringed at his acknowledgement of Tristan as his son.

"Hey, come check it out!" he told Paris.

"Uh, all right," she answered. She moved to the passenger door on the driver's side and reached for the handle.

"Hey! You can sit up front wit me, shorty! I ain't gon bite!"

Paris feigned a smile. "I will. I just want to check out the whole car," she told him.

"Everything's under control now, Mr. Detective!" Scotty told

Detective Hengess, shooing him away from the car.

Before another word could be uttered by anyone, a thunderous wail poured forth from the backseat. The exploding scream from her sister told Milan everything. Without hesitation she hurled her petite body into the front seat of the car. Scotty was hit so fast that he never even had a second to react. Both Detective Hengess and Blade immediately began trying to separate her from Scotty, while Aunt Millie poked her head into the backseat and saw what her niece's booming cry had already confirmed. Paris had fallen face down on the back seat, her eyes over-flooding with massive tears. Aunt Millie was trying to coax her from the car.

Scotty was trying to claw his way out the car through the other door, while at the same time defend himself against the sudden rage from his attacker.

"Milan, don't!" Blade pleaded, doing his very best to pull her from the front seat. Detective Hengess had made the wise decision to move to the other side of the car and attempt to rescue Scotty through the front passenger door.

Milan's arms were flailing all around the front seat. She managed to lock one of her hands onto Scotty's neck. Feeling his flesh beneath her fingers, the nails dug in forcefully. Scotty cried out in a voice raw with pain.

The Detective held onto one of Scotty's arms and was desperately trying to free him, while Scotty tried to fight her off with his other arm, as Milan clung mightily to his legs.

Sirens could now be heard in the distance as Detective Hengess had already requested the assistance of the Alpharetta Police Department since they were in their jurisdiction.

Finally, Blade was able to secure his arms around Milan's waist, which enabled him to yank her free from Scotty. She struggled to free herself from his grasp but then gave up, realizing that her diminutive body was no match against his.

Aunt Millie had also gotten Paris out of the car. Paris' head was buried into her Aunt's shoulder as she continued to sob uncontrollably.

Detective Hengess helped Scotty from the car through the front passenger's door. As he did so, several other police cars from the Alpharetta Police Department arrived on the scene.

Scotty could feel a wave of acid forming inside his stomach. Wild-eyed, he looked around at all the police cars. He turned an eye towards Milan but quickly averted his attention, unable to sustain her predatory expression. He had no idea what all this commotion was about. Neighbors had begun opening their doors, some peering through windows.

"For your own safety at the moment, Mister Sims, I'm gonna have you sit in one these cars," Detective Hengess told Scotty, escorting him to a nearby police car. The Detective told the officer that he wanted to have Scotty have a seat for a moment in his car while they sorted things out. The officer obliged.

Detective Hengess walked a few feet away from where Scotty had been seated and conferred with a Sergeant. He explained the situation, telling him that they might have a suspect on their hands that'd been involved in a carjacking and murder in the city of Atlanta back in the summer of 2002. The Sergeant had remembered the incident. Detective Hengess also shared how the twins believed that the Lexus they were standing next to had in fact been their father's Lexus due to some unique writing on the backseat.

A couple of other officers had ushered the twins, Aunt Millie and Blade back closer towards the house. Scotty refused to make eye contact with any of them.

Detective Hengess confirmed the words *grandpa* written on the back of the driver's seat headrest. It appeared to have been written by a child. He walked over to where Scotty was. "Mister Sims, are you the owner of this vehicle?" he asked, pointing to the Lexus.

Scotty grew nervous. "Uh . . . um, naw man. It ain't mine. I'm just keeping it for a buddy."

The Detective's eyes narrowed with suspicion. "Well, now Mister Sims. Didn't you just state a few moments ago that you wanted to make sure that – and I quote – 'nobody been tryin' to mess with *my* ride'?"

Scotty began to fidget. "Uh, don't I have a right to remain silent or something?"

Detective Hengess and the Sergeant exchanged enigmatic glances. "Well now, Mister Sims. That would be true if you were under arrest. And right now you have not been placed "under arrest. I'm simply asking you a few questions to try and sort this situation out."

While they had been talking, another officer called in the license plates on the car. He walked over to Detective Hengess and whispered something into his ear. The Detective's eyebrows arched.

"Please step from the car, Mister Sims," the Detective ordered.

Slowly, Scotty removed himself from the back seat of the police car.

"We have a little problem," he began. "First, let me remind you that I have witness you remove car keys from your pocket and unlock the doors to this vehicle. I have also witness you stating that the vehicle belonged to you. Now, we've just run a check on the plates and they don't match the car, Mister Sims. Would you care to explain why that is?"

"I told you, it ain't my car," Scotty said, as he began to feel the walls closing in.

"May I see the registration for this vehicle?" the Detective asked.

Scotty shifted from one foot to the other. "Uh, like I just told you, it ain't my car. So, how am I supposed to know anything about the registration?"

Frustrated, the Detective walked over to the vehicle. He plopped down on the front passenger seat and popped open the glove compartment. There was a small leather portfolio inside that contained the owner's manual to the car, there were also some receipts for service work, and then there was the registration. He pulled it out and examined it. It had expired. But more surprising than that was who the LEXUS LS430 had been registered to.

Detective Hengess emitted a heavy sign as he exited the vehicle. He showed the registration to the Sergeant. They exchanged a few words amongst themselves. Then the Sergeant walked over to Scotty.

"Mister Sims, you are being placed under arrest for possession of a stolen vehicle . . ."

"Hey, wait a minute!" Scotty shouted.

"Sir, you have the right to remain silent. Anything that you do say may be used against you in a court of law. You have "the right to consult an attorney before speaking to the police and to have an attorney present during questioning now or in the future . . ."

"But I ain't done nothing wrong!" Scotty yelled, as another officer had him turn around and face the police car while he patted him down.

The Sergeant continued with the reading of the *Miranda Rights*, "If you cannot afford an attorney, one will be appointed for you before any questioning if you wish."

Watching from the walkway in front of the house as the silver handcuffs were snapped onto Scotty's wrists, Paris and Milan made an attempt to venture over to him, but an officer held them at bay.

Aunt Millie glanced down the street and saw Nikki running towards them with Tristan at her heels. She'd been forced to park away from the house because so many police cars were blocking the street. Her face was stricken with horror as she saw Paris and Milan clinging to one another crying hysterically.

"I don't want Tristan to see all this!" Aunt Millie shouted, as she ran towards Nikki. When she reached them, she quickly shielded Tristan's view of the chaos with her body in front of him. She told Nikki to take him away. Nikki had wanted to know what was going on, but Aunt Millie just told her to call the house in a few minutes. "Right now, just get this child out of here!" she told Nikki.

Nikki rushed back to her car with Tristan at her side. He, too, had begun to ask questions about all the police cars, why his mommy and Auntie were crying and why the police were putting Mister Scotty into one of the police cars?

"Everything's going to be okay, big guy," Nikki assured him as she strapped the seatbelt onto him. But at the moment, even she had a difficult time believing her own words.

CHAPTER
TWENTY-FIVE

Sydney Salinas was relaxing in his hotel room and checking e-mail messages from his cell phone. The rain had started to pour over the city again on Saturday afternoon. Sounds from the television in the room seemed to be doing battle with the pounding noise of the rain against the windows. He was paying little attention to either.

Every now and then his eyes would glance over at the TV screen before quickly returning to the tiny screen on his cell phone. Since there would not be any golf today he'd decided to try and catch an early flight back to Dallas. He was able to find an open seat on AMERICAN for later this evening. This should bring a smile to his mother, he thought. But he decided not to tell her that he was in fact coming home today instead of tomorrow.

Sydney had spent a good part of the day thinking about Paris Alexander. He had been drawn to her since the first time that her beautiful face flashed across the television screen at his home several months ago. And when his mother had asked him to begin tracking their ad agency for future business interests, he certainly tried to shield his excitement.

While both sisters were equally gorgeous and quite personable, Paris had captured his heart like no one had ever done before. Being next to her gave him this incredible exhilaration that he really couldn't explain. When she spoke it was as if she were exhaling a breath of fresh air to those who were privileged to be in her presence.

His mother, however, seemed determined to keep him as a single man for the rest of his life. Sydney understood that he was her little boy. But his mother could be overwhelming at times, especially when it came to women that he had an interest in.

The cell phone suddenly dropped onto the desk. His eyes had made another glance towards the television. The words *Breaking News* flashed in large red letters across the screen. Scores of microphones from the media were being thrust into the faces of Milan and Paris. Sydney jumped from the chair and bolted over to the television to turn up the volume. Both sisters were refusing comment at the moment. A reporter on the scene began to summarize what had occurred, for the "benefit of those just tuning in".

Sydney would learn that the police had arrested a suspect in the carjacking and murder of Everson Alexander. As his heart began to race within him, he couldn't help but think about Paris and Milan.

As the news camera zoomed in on the twins' faces, a tall black gentleman quickly step in and rushed the sisters into a house that they'd been standing in front of.

Sydney, already clad in jeans and a T-shirt, grabbed a pair of loafers and slipped them on his bare feet. He made a quick call to the hotel's front desk and requested to have a taxi as soon as possible. As he frantically searched the room for his wallet, he dialed Paris' home number. Fortunately, he had programmed her home telephone number into his cell phone when she'd given it to him the other evening. After several rings with no answer, he ended the call. His wallet was found beneath the morning's USA TODAY. He stuffed it into the back pocket of his jeans and dashed from the room, sprinting towards the elevators with all the speed and determination of a track athlete competing for the gold medal in the Olympics.

CHAPTER
TWENTY-SIX

After he'd climbed into the backseat of the taxi, Sydney realized that he did not know the home address for Paris or Milan. During their dinner earlier in the week he remembered that Paris had told him that she lived in *Alpha-something*. But he couldn't quite recall the name of the area. He did, however, remember that she'd shared with him her often eventful drives home on Georgia Highway 400 north, so that was where he told the taxi driver to start the journey.

As they drove along the highway, he finally got through to Paris' home telephone number. The twins' Aunt Millie answered the phone. Sydney had met her at the office during his visit this past week. He explained to her that he had seen what had happened on the news and was heading their way, but he needed the address. After checking with Paris first and getting the okay, Aunt Millie gave Sydney the address. Fortunately, they were only a couple of exits away.

When the taxi came to a stop in front of the house there was no place to park because local media crews were still on the scene. They were positioned at various locations in front of the townhouse. There appeared to be one cameraman and one reporter for each of Atlanta's four major television stations, all beaming their stories back to their respective studios. And since the twins' sudden rise to fame had drawn national attention, CNN and FOX were also among the crews.

Sydney told the driver to just let him out of the cab where it had already stopped. He quickly retrieved some bills from his wallet and handed it over the seat to the driver, telling him to keep the change. The driver nodded and smiled at such a generous tip.

The reporters took notable interest as Sydney scampered across the street and up the walkway to the front door. As he rang the doorbell a reporter shouted a question to him. "Sir, are you a member of the family?"

Sydney turned toward the reporter, "I'm a business associate and friend," he kindly answered.

"Can you tell us anything about the arrest?" another reported shouted.

Sydney nodded, "No, I cannot." He pressed the doorbell again, hoping that the door would open soon.

"Sir, what is your *business* with the Alexander twins?"

Growing irritated, Sydney ignored the question. And as the overly inquisitive reporter began to repeat the question, the front door opened and the tall black man that he'd seen moments earlier on the television screen yanked him inside the house, quickly shutting the door behind him as a swarm of reporters rushed forward.

"Sorry about that," the gentleman apologized. "But we thought it was the reporters. Over the past hour that doorbell has become as annoying as a telemarketer calling in the middle of dinner."

Sydney chuckled. "No problem."

"Everyone's in the other room," he said, leading him to a spare room that Paris had converted into an office. "Oh, by-the-way, I'm *Blade Barnes.*"

"Of course. Paris mentioned your name to me. You were going to be the fourth member of our foursome today, right?"

"Yeah, too bad Mother Nature didn't cooperate!"

"I know. I was really looking forward it! Hey, I'm *Sydney Salinas.*"

The two men shook hands and then continued towards the other room.

When they arrived, Sydney saw Paris and Milan standing in one corner of the room speaking to a man in a trench coat. Their Aunt Millie was speaking with someone on the telephone. Upon his entrance all eyes turned towards him.

Paris didn't hide her enthusiasm as she rushed over to Sydney and threw her arms around him. He held her close, consoling her at the same time. Milan introduced him to Detective Hengess and she was about to do likewise with Blade, but the two men confirmed to her that they'd already exchanged greetings.

Detective Hengess wrapped up his discussion with the twins and Aunt Millie. He told them that he would make a brief statement to the media and that he'd have to make it clear to them that at the moment Scotty Sims had only been arrested for being in possession of a stolen vehicle.

After the detective departed the house, Paris explained to Sydney what had occurred. He told them all how sorry he was that they had to relive their father's tragedy. He also offered his support in any way that they might need it.

An hour later all was quiet outside Paris' home. The media trucks with the satellite antennas on top were gone. Their father's Lexus had been towed. And even the nosy neighbors had retreated inside their respective homes. Nikki had returned with Tristan – both were full of questions. Aunt Millie had taken Tristan to his room and put him down for a nap. It didn't take long for the six year-old to fall fast asleep.

When Aunt Millie returned downstairs she was surprised to see Paris still clinging to Sydney. She assumed that the two must have gotten quite close over the past week. Blade also had an arm wrapped around the waist of Milan. For a moment, it made her a little uncomfortable. "Well, I guess I'm going to leave you young folk some time to yourselves," she said, retrieving her jacket from the closet.

"Are you leaving Aunt Millie?" Paris asked.

"I'm afraid so. It's been an eventful day and I just need some time to myself," she answered.

"Are you going to be okay?" Milan was concerned.

Aunt Millie fanned the air with her hand. "Of course! I'll be just fine. You young folk don't need me hanging around all afternoon," she remarked, forcing a smile.

"Well now, Mildred. It's nice of you to include an old fogy like me amongst these youngsters!" Blade joked.

Aunt Millie smiled sheepishly. "Blade Barnes, you're still very much a young man."

Her comment caused him to blush. "Why, thank you Mildred. Your kind words just knocked another ten years or so off this forty-one year-old!"

Everyone laughed. "Yes, and it just added another twenty to his *ego!*" Milan piped, bringing on more laughter. Blade gave her a friendly jab with his elbow.

"Like they say – age ain't nothing but a number, right?" Sydney said.

"Yeah, that is what they say," Paris concurred.

"Well, I can't wait until I turn twenty-one," Nikki remarked.

"Honey, don't rush it," Aunt Millie advised. "You need to enjoy every stage of your life. I mean age is a journey. We're all passing through from one bracket to the next. No one settles into a certain age and remain there forever. So, while you're eighteen enjoy it and then be prepared to move on, because your age will move on whether you're ready or not."

Blade pumped his fist into the air. "I couldn't have said it any better myself!" he stated. "You're a very wise *young* woman, Mildred!"

They each praised Aunt Millie with kind words before she finally exited the front door.

The January air was slightly breezy, but the rain had stopped and a hint of the sun's presence behind the clouds was beginning to make itself known. She inhaled deeply and then quickly exhaled as she strolled down the driveway to her car, the wind caressing her cheeks ever so gently. She couldn't help but wonder if there'd ever come a time in her life when she would have someone to share a laugh, maybe an arm around the waist, or simply an elbow jab.

Turning the car's ignition, Aunt Millie then dabbed her eyes dry with the back of her hand. As the car's engine came to life, she switched on the wipers and watched nonchalantly as the raindrops quickly disappeared from the windshield. It occurred to her that that was just how quickly things could change in life. She'd experienced her fair share of heartache over the years. And none could equal losing her brother so tragically. For that, there was no *switch* to turn. Somehow she knew that the windshield of her eyes would be forever dotted with raindrops – raindrops of tears. And for these, nothing could so easily wipe them away.

CHAPTER
TWENTY-SEVEN

One week had passed since the arrest of Scotty Sims. After much interrogation, Scotty finally admitted to having been a part of the carjacking of Everson Alexander on that fateful August night. And while he had not been the triggerman in the incident, he fingered the other guy and agreed to testify against the shooter.

It would be learned that Scotty had been drinking heavily that night and had allowed himself to be talked into the carjacking by some thug that he'd only known two weeks prior. Their intent had been to only steal the car, joy ride for a little while and then strip it down and sell the parts. Once Everson had been pulled from the driver's seat at gunpoint, Scotty had jumped into the passenger seat of the car. He watched through the window as Everson had struggled with the gunman. When the gunman broke free he immediately fired two shots into Everson's head, killing him instantly. Scotty had no idea that the person they were carjacking was Everson Alexander.

The gunman drove the car to a sleazy garage on the south side of the city. A week later it had been painted black. They had intended to try and sell the car, but the gunman was arrested a few days later on some other charges for which he would be convicted. Scotty didn't have a car at the time so he simply took ownership of the car. He never once looked inside the glove compartment to view the registration papers. When the time had come to get new license plates he simply paid someone for stolen plates and slapped them on the car. And since he actually drove the car, he never noticed the words *grandpa* scribbled on the back of the headrest. He'd had many friends sitting in the backseat of the car, but they were either too stoned or too drunk to even notice.

His cooperation with the prosecutor by agreeing to testify against the triggerman, who was already serving time in a Federal prison for other crimes, would help his own case, but it was unlikely that he would escape jail time.

The trial was slated to begin some time in late spring or early summer. Neither Milan nor Paris intended on going to the trial. However, Aunt Millie made it clear to her nieces that she would definitely be right there in the court room – front and center – every single day that the trial was in session, to make sure that both thugs got what they deserved.

Understandably, the twins wanted closure. And now that an arrest had been made they were confident that justice would be served.

Paris vowed to never tell Tristan about Scotty. There was simply nothing to be gained by doing so.

The twins were eager to redirect their focus on saving their father's advertising agency. And if that meant merging with another agency to overcome their current plight then that was what they would do.

Since his initial visit to Atlanta, Sydney had made two additional trips. They were yet to meet his mother, Mirabella Salinas, but they had spoken with her via a conference call. Lawyers from both sides were currently working on terms and conditions of the merger, which was scheduled to close some time in early to mid-March.

The press was also aware of the pending merger. Some taunted it as the twins being rescued from an impending financial disaster, while others reported that the sisters were to be praised for recognizing a business opportunity that would eventually benefit both agencies. But the twins didn't allow the negative press coverage to worry them. They were ready to take on any challenge presented to them.

Mirabella Salinas, on the other hand, had worries of a much different kind.

CHAPTER
TWENTY-EIGHT

Valentine's day was still four days away, so when Belinda arrived at Paris' office with the large bouquet of peach roses her thoughts centered immediately on Sydney. It had been about six weeks since she'd first met him and the two of them had fallen deeply for one another.

Milan, of course, was constantly *advising* her to take matters slowly, especially since the merger with Sydney's ad agency had not been completed. Both were keenly aware of their need to be discrete and were therefore trying very hard to maintain a professional atmosphere whenever Sydney visited their offices. And as far as Paris knew, no one at the agency suspected anything was going on between she and Sydney, with the exception of Aunt Millie.

Paris was gazing, with a gleam in her eyes, at the two-dozen roses that were neatly arranged in a crystal vase and setting in the center of her desk. She absolutely adored roses of all sorts. She knew that the color *peach* conveyed desire or anticipation. Peach roses also generally signified *sincere appreciation* and *optimism* for future endeavors. She was certainly very optimistic about her future with Sydney Salinas, and apparently he shared the same sentiments.

Turning the vase around, she retrieved the small card that was tucked amongst the beautiful flowers. Opening the envelope, she pulled out the card and read: *I HAVE ALWAYS ADMIRED YOU!* It was signed with the letters *J-R-I-L-Y.*

Paris smiled. Sydney enjoyed teasing her. She glanced at her watch. The time was just after two o'clock. The time in Dallas was one hour behind. She hoped that Sydney was in the office as she dialed his direct number.

Thanks to caller ID he could see her number displayed on his telephone's LCD screen. "Hello, my Princess!" Sydney answered.

Paris blushed. "Hello yourself, my Knight in shining armor!"

He chuckled. "Oh, you're just saying that because I'm buying your agency," he joked.

"I am not," Paris retorted.

"Really? Then why dost thou callest me *thy Knight in shining armor?*"

Paris couldn't contain her laughter. "First of all, you silly boy, I never used the word 'thy'; and secondly, I consider you *my* Knight – not because you're rescuing the ALEXANDER AGENCY, but because you've rescued my *heart.*"

"I have?"

"Yes, you have."

"Well, glad that I could be of service, Miss Alexander."

"Is that all you have to say, Mister Salinas?"

"Uh, would you like me to say more?"

Paris cleared her throat. "This is the part where you're supposed to tell me how I've also rescued your heart, blah blah blah."

He chuckled again. "Oh, right! Well, I'd like to tell you that you stole my heart, Miss Alexander, but that wouldn't quite be true."

"Why not?"

He exhaled. "Well, the truth of the matter is that you didn't have to *steal* my heart . . . the day that I first laid eyes upon you I *surrendered* it – freely, willingly."

There was a moment of silence from Paris' end of the telephone. She'd begun to stifle a small band of tears that were beginning to surround her eyelids. "You are the sweetest, Sydney."

He could hear her sniffles. "I didn't intend to make you cry. I'm sorry."

"Don't be," she told him. "When it comes to tears I'm just like a river – full and flowing!"

"Well, if the Good Lord didn't intend for us to cry then I suppose he wouldn't have given us tears, right?"

"Yeah, and sometimes I think He gave me an extra measure because He knew that I would be so generous with them."

Sydney laughed out loud.

"Hey, by the way, thanks so much for these beautiful peach roses," Paris said.

Sydney's eyebrows arched. "Roses?"

"Oh, don't even try it!"

Sydney had been leaning back in his leather chair with his feet atop his desk. His feet dropped to the floor as he sat up straight. "You received roses today?"

"Two dozen to be exact."

He swallowed hard. "Tengo cierta competición."

"Does that mean *you're welcome* or something? I mean I only know three Spanish terms – *uno, dos* and *tres*."

Sydney smiled, while thinking to himself just how lucky he was to have met this goddess. "Uh, all I said was that *I have some competition.*"

"What do you mean, 'competition'?"

"Paris, I didn't send you those flowers."

"Are you being serious?"

"Unfortunately, I am."

"Then who sent them?" she asked, not really expecting him to provide the answer.

"Your guess is as good as mine. Was there a card?"

"Yeah, there was. But it was sort of vague."

"What did it say?"

She retrieved the card again. "It just says that *'I have always admired you'* and then it's signed at the bottom with the letters J-R-I-L Y."

Sydney ran his fingers through his dark wavy hair. "Sounds to me like you might have a secret admirer."

"Oh, please."

"No kidding, Paris. I've met your agency's staff remember? And I recall quite a few good-looking guys there who'd probably love nothing more than to win your affection."

"Well, I don't date my employees."

"Perhaps. But guys can be persistent."

She allowed the card to fall to the desk. "It doesn't matter. I have no romantic interest in the guys that work here. In fact, I haven't had a serious relationship since Scotty."

Sydney found this bit of information surprising. "You haven't dated since you broke up with your son's father?"

"I didn't say that I haven't *dated*. I said that I haven't had a *serious* relationship."

"Oh."

"That's why I said that you've rescued my heart. I'm very happy when I'm around you or just talking to you over the phone."

"I feel the same way, Paris. But I'd be lying if I said that I wasn't feeling a little insecure right now."

"Why? Because of the flowers?"

"Well, they didn't just fall from the sky!"

"I know that. But honestly, I don't have a clue who sent me these roses."

"Well, maybe your other *Knight* will reveal himself soon."

"Ha, ha, very funny."

The two talked a little while longer before Sydney had to end the call and prepare for an afternoon meeting.

Paris sat at her desk staring at the gorgeous blooms. A thought occurred to her. She dialed the receptionist's station. "Hi, Belinda. It's me. Do you know if these flowers that I received were delivered by a florist?"

"Yes. When the security desk had called I asked Sabrina to go down and escort the delivery guy up," Belinda answered, referring to one the agency's administrative assistants. "This switchboard was going crazy!"

"Um, do you remember which florist it was?"

"Let's see . . . as a matter of fact the guy was wearing a cap with their name and logo on it." She closed her eyes in an attempt to visualize the name. "I believe the name was SCENTED PETALS or something like that."

"Well, when you have a free moment give them a call and see if you can find out who sent me these flowers, okay?"

"There wasn't a card attached?"

"There was one, but it was pretty vague."

"All right. No problem. I'll see what I can do."

"Thanks Belinda."

Paris moved the vase from her desk and set it in the center of her coffee table. She couldn't deny that they were definitely beautiful. As she began to arrange the stems she tried to figure out just who could have sent them, and more importantly *why*?

Her telephone began ringing. Paris scurried back to her desk. "This is Paris," she answered.

"Hi, Paris. It's Belinda."

"Hey, you got the information already?"

"Oh, no. Not yet. I haven't got to it. I was calling to let you know that your son's school is on hold for you."

Not again, Paris thought. "Please tell that teacher that I'm in a meeting or something. I really don't want to talk to her right now."

"Um, it's not your son's teacher, Paris. It's the school nurse."

Her heart immediately began to beat faster. "Oh god. Put it through!"

The line could barely ring before Paris quickly depressed the button to answer the call. "This is Miss Alexander."

The very polite nurse from Tristan's school identified herself. She was calling because Tristan had fallen while on the playground. Apparently he and some other boys were chasing each other and Tristan tripped and fell. The nurse explained that Tristan wasn't seriously injured, but that he did have a couple of scratches on his arm. Paris asked how he was doing and she told her that he was all right, especially now that the scratches had been cleaned and a Band-Aid had been placed on one of the scratches.

Paris was relieved. Although the injury was minor, it was the school's policy to notify parents of any such incidents involving their child. After finishing her call with the school nurse she phoned Nikki and told her what had happened so that when she picked Tristan up from school she would understand why he had a Band-Aid on his arm.

There was a knock at her door.

"Come in," she answered. It was Milan.

"Hey there, Sis."

"Hey, girl."

"Wow! Sydney's getting an early start on Valentine's Day

"isn't he?" Milan asked, noticing the roses.

"They're not from Sydney."

Milan eyed her skeptically. "They're not?"

"Nope," Paris answered simply. She opened a file and pretended to become engrossed in the file's content.

"Don't ignore me, Paris."

"I'm not ignoring you," she stated, continuing to peruse the file.

"Well, if it wasn't Sydney then who?"

She shrugged her shoulders. "Not that it's any of your business, but I don't know who sent them. Satisfied?"

Milan sat on a corner of her sister's desk. "I'll bet I know who sent them?"

Paris smacked the folder shut. "Okay, Miss Know-It-All! Who sent them?"

"Naoko Jackson!"

"Oh, give it a rest, Milan," Paris responded. Although the thought had crossed her mind as well. "Naoko isn't interested in me like that and I'm certainly not interested in him romantically."

"Well, you may not have an interest in him, but I've been trying to tell you for months now that the man has a crush on you!"

"Please! Our relationship has always been strictly professional and you know that."

Milan rolled her eyes. "Remember that Christmas gift he gave you?"

"Yeah, and the key word here is *Christmas* gift!"

"Paris, the man bought you designer perfume!"

"So what? It's no secret that I love designer fragrances."

"Sis, don't be so naive."

While Paris did her best to defend herself against her sister's accusations, she was beginning to wonder if whether or not Milan was far off base. Now that she thought about it, Naoko had been stopping by her office more lately – smiling, being overly friendly. Maybe he did have a crush on her.

Paris realized that there was only one thing to do. She'd have to confront Naoko. If in fact he did send her those flowers then he had some serious explaining to do.

CHAPTER
TWENTY-NINE

Naoko Jackson was visibly nervous as he walked down the corridor towards Paris Alexander's office. He was wondering if this would be the day that he'd dreamed of ever since he joined the ad agency.

Sending her those flowers had not been an easy decision for him. He'd agonized over it all weekend long before finally deciding yesterday to have the florist deliver them. And while he had seriously considered sending her red roses, he decided to save that bouquet for a more important occasion.

Naoko was fully aware of the fact that Paris was his boss. And although he understood that many companies often frowned upon dating in the workplace, he knew that his situation was different – at least to *him* it was.

Whether or not Paris was already involved with someone was unbeknownst to him. Though he was inclined to believe that she was single and available. It was his intuition that led him to believe that she was a *free* woman. After all, he hadn't seen any guys dropping by the office lately to take her to lunch. And there was certainly no ring on her pretty little finger.

One of the creative directors had told him the other day that he was quite sure Paris was seeing that Latino guy who'd been visiting their offices a lot lately. But, at a staff meeting recently, his identity and presence around the office had been made clear. The agency was in the process was being bought by some Dallas-based ad agency and thus it had been explained to the staff that over the next several weeks there might be some unfamiliar faces around the offices. Apparently this Latino dude was one of the higher-ups.

Naoko wasn't worried. The guy didn't appear to be Paris' type anyway. Not that she had told him what her type was.

Arriving at her office he knocked on the door softly. She invited him in and asked him to close the door behind him. He complied.

"You wanted to see me?" Naoko spoke, as he wondered if the perspiration drops falling from his armpits were as audible to her as they were in his ears.

"I did. Please, just have a seat," she answered, pointing to one of the chairs positioned in front of her desk.

Naoko sat carefully, unsure of whether to rest his arms on the chair's armrests or simply on his lap. He eventually chose the armrests. His heart was still beaming from noticing the roses setting on her coffee table when he'd walked into the office – a sure sign that she liked them.

"How's your day been, Naoko?" Paris asked, unsure of how to broach this subject matter.

He grinned and nodded fiercely. "It's been all good! Just finishing some copy ideas that I've been working on."

"Well, let me say that your work here is excellent! And you have always been a big help to me. I mean I didn't have the creative background that you do when I came onboard, but thanks to your willingness to tutor me along the way, I've learned a lot over the past year and half."

"Thanks, Paris. You catch on real fast!"

She forced a smile. "Unfortunately, Naoko, we're not meeting to discuss your work performance."

He shifted his posture in the chair.

"I need to ask you some personal questions, if you don't mind?"

"Hey, I'll answer whatever I can for you, Paris."

"Well, that's very much appreciated."

"Fire away!"

She leaned back in her chair. "Naoko, how do you feel about me?"

For months he'd practiced answering such a question from

her, but all of a sudden he'd become speechless. His mind had apparently gone blank. "Uh . . . um, you're good," he heard himself answer. What! That was his answer? *You're good* – what in the heck did that mean? Attempting to try and save face he quickly added, "I mean I like you, Paris." Whew! He'd said it. That was a much better response.

"Like me how?"

Okay, calm down Naoko. Calm the heck down!

"Um, you know . . . you're a great person."

Paris had never seen him so nervous before. "I think I might be putting you on the spot so I'll . . ."

He interrupted her, "No, no, no. I don't feel like I'm being put on the spot at all. I'm just a little tongue-tied that's all."

"Well, let me hopefully make it easier by cutting to the chase. Naoko, did you send me those flowers?" She pointed to the vase behind him on the coffee table.

For a brief moment he considered lying. Tell her that he'd never seen those flowers before in his life. That he was in fact allergic to flowers – especially roses! *Peach* roses being the worst! He didn't know why he'd considered lying. It had never dawned upon him that she might take offense at his innocent gesture. Or that maybe *she* was allergic to flowers! Oh god, what had he done? This was turning out to be third grade all over again. Once, in elementary school, at recess, he'd picked a handful of flowers and given them to this very pretty girl whom he liked. Well, the *flowers* turned out to be *poison ivy*. Both his skin and hers became inflamed and littered with itching blisters. Needless to say, when he and the girl returned to school, several days later, she never spoke to him again.

Realizing that she was awaiting his answer, he finally replied, "Yes." Then he braced himself for her wrath that he was certain would come at any second.

"Well, thank you. They're very lovely. But I have to ask you why did you send me roses?"

"Oh, you'd prefer some other flower?"

"It's not about my preference. I love roses, especially peach. But what I mean is, for what reason did you send them to *me*?"

He shifted his posture again. "Uh, I guess I just wanted to,"

Naoko answered dryly. "I mean, you've been through a lot lately and . . . well, I just wanted to try and brighten your day."

"I appreciate your thoughtfulness, Naoko. I really do. But I want to make sure that you understand our relationship . . ." She paused. He was giving her his full attention. "I'm your employer. Now I'm not saying that at the same time we can't be friends, but our relationship is a professional one, okay?"

His feet might just as well have been secured in cement blocks and his body dumped into the Atlantic because that's just how fast his heart sank within him. "Could we ever move beyond just *friends* and *professionalism*?" he asked solemnly.

Paris shook her head. "I'm sorry, Naoko."

"Is it me personally or what?"

"Of course not. It has nothing to do with you. It's the situation we're in."

"The fact that you're my boss, huh?"

She nodded again.

He stood from the chair. "Hey, no need to say anything more. I understand what you're saying."

"Are you sure you're okay with everything?"

Naoko balled his hand into a fist and beat it against his heart. "I feel you, Paris." Then he told her that he had to get back to work.

After he'd left her office, with an obvious pained expression across his face, Paris plopped her head onto her desk. It had not been her intention to hurt his feelings. She berated herself for not nipping this whole thing in the bud much sooner when Milan told her that he had a crush on her.

While still commiserating the situation she heard Belinda's voice pipe through the telephone's intercom. She lifted her head slowly from the desk and picked up the receiver. "Hey there."

"Paris, I spoke with the florist and they said that the sender of those flowers requested to remain anonymous and . . ."

"Don't worry about it, Belinda," Paris interrupted. "I've already found out who sent them." She clicked the phone off before Belinda could say anything else. At the moment she was wishing that she could make a request to someone and request anonymity for herself.

CHAPTER
THIRTY

Flower Mound, Texas is just twenty-eight miles northwest of downtown Dallas. With a population over fifty thousand it is home to one of Dallas' top advertising executives – fifty-three year-old Mirabella Salinas. The former runway model shares her 9,000 square feet of living space with her two Shih Tzu dogs – *Dooney* and *Bourke*.

Mirabella's $3 million dollar mansion sits on two spacious, tree-lined acres that backs into a thirty-six-hole golf course. The domicile boasts intricate details throughout. Though she rarely entertains guests in her home, the formal dining room plays host to a fourteen-foot round table that can seat sixteen. And the sophisticated two-story library is her sanctuary away from the office.

It was in the library on this Thursday evening where Mirabella was sitting on the sofa. Dooney was resting comfortably on her lap as she lightly stroked his fur with her right hand while holding a glass of Merlot in her left hand. Both dogs usually clung to her like newborn infants. But lately, Bourke was more aloof, wandering about the house keeping to himself. She knew that his behavior change was primarily her fault. She'd allowed herself to become preoccupied with this agency acquisition. And of course, with Sydney allowing his personal feelings to enter into the situation, that didn't help matters at all. She should have assigned the task to someone else instead of placing her boy in harms way.

The doorbell began chiming. Mirabella set down the glass of Merlot on a nearby table and rose from the sofa with Dooney snuggled in her arms. She'd been awaiting the arrival of Sydney. And although she had told him that she wanted to discuss the progress of their pending acquisition of the ALEXANDER AGENCY, she realized that there were more important matters that needed to be discussed with him as well. Matters that seemed to be getting out of control.

"Hello, son!" she greeted him as she opened the door. She kissed him on the cheek.

"Hello, mother," he greeted, returning a kiss to her.

"Why didn't you use key? You still have it don't you?" she questioned, closing the door.

"Yes, I still have it. But this is your home, mother. I'm not going to just let myself in any time I want simply because I have a key."

"That is why I give it to you, Sydney."

"I know, mother. But I want to respect your privacy as well."

Mirabella restrained a laugh as they walked through the marbled foyer towards the library. "What privacy? You think I bring some man into my home?"

When they reached the library Bourke scampered into the room as well. Sydney quickly picked him up. "Hi there little fella! What have you been up to?"

"Do not try and change subject, Sydney," Mirabella warned, resuming her seat on the sofa. "Now tell me, do you really think I could be with another man after your father?"

Sydney sat down beside his mother, still holding Bourke. "Mother, you deserve to be happy. Dad's been gone a long time now. He knew how much you loved him. And I know how much you loved him. But I also know that he would not want you to just let your life drift away."

She took offense at his words. "Is that what you think of your mother? That her life is just drifting away?"

"Oh, mother. You know what I mean."

"No! I do not know! What you mean my life drift away? Am I not hard worker, Sydney? Am I not care for you? Explain to me what you are talking about!"

Sydney suddenly realized that there had to be something

else going on with his mother. He put Bourke down on the floor and moved closer to his mother. "What's really going on, mother?"

She looked away from her son's face. Sydney touched the bottom of her chin and gently turned her head towards him again. "Talk to me, mother."

Mirabella's beautiful ageless features had now fallen. Her eyes were incurably sad, obviously haunted by some inner pain. Sydney had never seen his mother look this way. His heart grew anxious. He removed Dooney from her arms and set him on the floor as well. Taking hold of her hands he squeezed them softly. "I'm here for you, mother. Please, talk to me."

Unable to restrain her emotions, Mirabella dropped her head and began to weep. Sydney put his arms around her and held her close to him, stroking her long black hair. "It's all right, mother. Whatever it is, everything will be all right."

CHAPTER
THIRTY-ONE

Two hours after his arrival, Sydney and his mother were sitting quietly in the grand room. He sipped on a cup of hot chocolate while Mirabella nursed a new glass of Merlot. The two of them had just devoured her homemade chili and *Jiffy* cornbread. The meal was quite fitting for Dallas' cool thirty-three-degrees, which had taken a turn for the worse after pleasant temperatures were recorded earlier in the week. But outside the palatial home this evening the winds were blowing loud and steady like notes from a trumpet in the hands of a jazz musician. The soft crackling of wood burning in the room's stone fireplace filled the occasional void when neither of them uttered a word.

"So, Eduardo tells me that the acquisition should happen very soon," Mirabella stated, breaking another round of silence. Eduardo was their corporate attorney.

"Mmm, that's right," Sydney answered, swallowing a large sip of the soothing liquid that was laden with marshmallows. "If all goes well, the deal should close on March first."

"So soon?" Mirabella remarked with surprise. "That's only a couple of weeks away!"

"Mother, I was under the impression that you wanted this deal done quickly."

"Well . . . I do. It's just that . . . well, I thought it would take much longer."

"We've been working on this since early January. Besides,

"it has been Milan and Paris who've helped to speed things along."

Mirabella stiffened at the mention of the Alexander twins. "Well, I'm not surprised. They appear to be very bright young women."

"Oh, mother! You have to meet them!" Sydney exclaimed. "They are quite anxious to meet you!"

She took a long sip from her glass. "Well, I'm sure I'll get to meet them very soon."

Sydney set his cup atop the fireplace mantle and trotted enthusiastically over to his mother, who'd been reclining across the room in a winged-back chair. He kneeled on the floor beside her. "Mother, why don't you fly to Atlanta with me tomorrow and meet them? I'm sure they'd love to have you!"

Mirabella smiled thinly while at the same time attempting to shield her nervousness. "I didn't know you were going there tomorrow."

"Oh. Well, this trip is personal not business."

"Meaning?"

He rose to his feet and sat on the arm of the chair. "Meaning that I'm planning to take Paris out to dinner for Valentine's Day on Saturday."

Suddenly her cheeks felt like they were bloated, as if holding back vomit. She set her glass down and brushed strands of hair from her eye. "Sydney, forgive me for saying this, but I don't think you should involve yourself personally with her."

"What are you talking about, mother? Paris and I care very much for each other. And I'm beginning to think that she's the one."

Instinctively Mirabella sprang from the chair. "No!" she screamed, her voice penetrating the art-framed walls. At the moment her head was spinning wildly. She didn't know if it was a result of the Merlot or the realization of what was happening around her.

"Calm down, mother," Sydney told her, walking up behind her. "Why should my personal involvement with Paris concern you and cause you to react like this?"

She turned around and faced him. "Sydney, this was supposed to be *business* transaction! Nothing more, nothing "less! I did not send you to Atlanta to fall in love!"

As Sydney stared into his mother's beautiful green eyes, he tried assiduously to search them for clues as to what it was that his mother was obviously keeping from him. He knew how protective she could be, but he'd never seen her respond like this to his interest in any woman – and he'd brought home his fair share over the past few years. "Mother, is there something about Paris that you don't like?"

"Of course not!" she answered quickly, resuming her position in the winged-back chair. "I mean I never meet her."

Sydney knelt beside her again. "Then mother, I'm asking you . . . please, trust me on this, okay?"

Admittedly, Mirabella couldn't remember the last time that she'd seen her son's face light up at the mere mention of a woman's name. She had no doubt that he was in love with Paris Alexander. She realized that Sydney was a smart boy who'd grown to become an intelligent man. And under normal circumstances she wouldn't be as adamant or vocal with regards to her son's personal life. But circumstances were not *normal*. She had her reasons for wanting to buy the ALEXANDER AGENCY. Equally so, she now have her reasons for wanting to keep her son from making perhaps the biggest *mistake* of his life.

CHAPTER
THIRTY-TWO

Every Friday morning some of the employees from the ALEXANDER AGENCY gathered at 7:00 A.M. in the main conference room for their weekly *Reality Ruckus* – an informal roundtable discussion on the latest happenings from current reality television shows. To aid in the functioning of their brains at the early hour, KRISPY KREMES, coffee and orange juice were plentiful. Milan, a reality TV fanatic, rarely missed a meeting. Paris, however, showed up occasionally. Both were in attendance on this Friday the thirteenth.

"Hey, where's Naoko?" Paris asked, looking around the room at the fifteen or so employees who'd made the session. "I thought he was a regular contributor!"

"I haven't seen him this morning," one of the account executives answered. "He's usually here every week."

The hot topic of the morning was last night's reality show, THE APPRENTICE. Once the ruckus began, opinions flew back and forth across the table like ping pong balls.

"Can you believe the nerve of Omarosa?" Milan shouted, taking control of the discussion.

"I know!" answered a female media planner. "Even Trump was surprised by what she said about Heidi!"

"She'd never last a day in this agency," another female executive quipped.

"Well, I agree with what Carolyn had to say about her," Paris added. "Omarosa has absolutely no leadership qualities "whatsoever! I mean the woman does more talking about her resume than anything else!"

"What do you all think about Jessie being fired?" Milan asked.

One of the three men in the group spoke. "Hey, I'm just glad to see the men dodging the firing bullets for a change!"

The room erupted into laughter.

"Yeah, the women were kicking y'alls behinds for awhile there!" Belinda interjected.

"Well, although I agree that Jessie was the weakest one last night, I still would have preferred to see Omarosa get the boot," Milan stated.

"Her time is coming soon!" someone else said.

"Definitely!" echoed another.

"I think Kwame is her only ally," Milan's assistant said.

"The brother better watch his back!" noted one of the men.

"I heard that!" Belinda agreed. "Omarosa isn't someone I'd trust to throw me a life preserver."

As the morning time dwindled towards eight o'clock, the group moved on to other reality shows that had aired within the past week, like AMERICAN IDOL and AMERICA'S NEXT TOP MODEL. Those discussions were equally rousing.

Later that morning, Paris took a stroll across the floor to see Aunt Millie. When she arrived her door was locked and no one answered when she knocked. She left and decided to stop by Milan's office to see if she knew their Aunt's whereabouts.

Milan was typing on the computer when she reached her office. The door was open so Paris walked in and over to her sister. "Hey, girl. What's up?"

Milan swiveled around in her chair. "Hi there, Sis. I was just revising my thoughts for the press release."

"Press release?"

"Yes. The one we'll be putting out once this merger is complete next month."

"Yeah, right. I appreciate you agreeing to handle that part," Paris told her. "I don't like dealing with the media."

"Well, neither do I. But at least this will be something positive."

Paris sat in one of her sister's desk chairs. "You know, we

"keep calling this thing a merger when actually it's really an acquisition."

"I know. Blade pointed that out to me the other day. But you know what? It doesn't matter. As long as we're able to keep this agency afloat then I'm happy."

Paris smiled. "Yeah, I guess that's what's most important." She then remembered the reason for her visit to her sister's office. "Hey, do you know where Aunt Millie is? I just came from her office and the door is locked and she didn't answer when I knocked."

Stuffing some files into her desk drawer, Milan apologized. "I'm sorry that I forgot to tell you, but she phoned me last night and said that she was taking the day off."

"Is she okay?"

"Oh, of course. She's going to go over to the house to start sorting through Daddy's belongings. You know the house is going on the market some time this spring."

Paris let out a deep sigh. "Yeah, I know. I guess we can't expect Aunt Millie to keep looking after the house forever. You know, I'm surprised that she won't just move in it."

"Paris, you know that house is too big for one person. I mean even though Daddy left it to us, neither of us wants to live in it either."

"Well, it wasn't the size that made me not want to live in it. There are just too many memories."

"Yeah, you're right. Maybe that's how Aunt Millie feels too."

"I suppose. She and Daddy were very close."

Intentionally changing the subject, Milan asked, "Sis, what do you have planned for Valentine's Day tomorrow?"

"Didn't I tell you? Sydney is flying in tonight and he's treating me to dinner at the SUNDIAL."

"You've been there before, haven't you?"

"Yeah, I know. But he hasn't."

"So, you two seem to be getting closer every day, huh?"

Paris smiled broadly, her eyes dancing with joy. "Things are getting a little serious," she answered.

"Well, Sydney is a nice guy. I'm happy for you, Sis." Milan stood from her chair and stretched across the desk to give her sister a warm hug.

"Thanks, girl. I haven't felt like this since Sco . . . well, in a "very long time."

Milan gave her sister a kiss on the cheek before sitting down again.

Paris decided to put her sister on the hot seat. "Why don't you tell me how you and Mister Barnes are doing these days?"

Milan waved off her question with a preemptory gesture.

"I'm serious!" Paris stated.

"Blade and I are just friends, okay?"

"Yeah, right. Friends with benefits!"

Milan chuckled. "Sis, you know it's not like that."

Paris shook her head. "I don't know a thing!"

Milan ignored her, swiveling her chair around to face her computer. She began to type on the keyboard.

"You gonna give me the silent treatment, huh? Well, just so you know – your silence is speaking volumes!"

Milan began to sing the song, WHITE FLAG, a track from DIDO's latest CD: "*I will go down with this ship, I won't put my hands up and surrender . . .*"

"Don't try and tune me out, Milan," Paris warned, quickly becoming annoyed at her sister.

Milan continued to sing, " *. . .There will be no white flag above my door . . .*"

Having had enough, Paris jumped from her chair and rushed to her sister's chair. She was about to place her hands over Milan's mouth to shut her up when a knock at the door startled them both. They turned around to find an elderly deliveryman standing at the entrance with a dozen red roses.

"Delivery for a Miss Alexander," he said.

"Which one?" they asked in unison.

For a moment the deliveryman looked puzzled, then seeing the uncanny similarity between the two women he realized the dilemma and quickly searched the bouquet for the card. Finding it, he read the name. "*Milan Alexander!*"

"That's me," Milan said, politely pushing her sister aside and walking over to retrieve the flowers.

"The woman at the front desk said it was okay to bring them to you," the deliveryman told her. "I think she had her hands full with the telephones."

"No problem. Thank you very much," Milan said.

The deliveryman gave her a smile before exiting her office.

Milan placed the flowers on her credenza right next to her computer, all the while trying to suppress an incriminating smile.

"Like I said, friends with benefits," Paris couldn't resist saying.

"Blade is very thoughtful," Milan responded. "Just like Naoko."

Paris rolled her eyes. "That little misunderstanding has been put to rest."

"Humph. I don't know if I'd call three dozen peach roses a *little misunderstanding*," Milan mocked.

"It was *two* dozen!" Paris corrected.

"So, you counted?"

"Milan, please. Just leave Naoko out of this."

"I will if you lay off Blade."

"Fine."

"Fine."

The twins stared each other down before breaking into laughter.

"You might want to get your little behind back to work before I have to pull a *Donald Trump* on you!" Milan teased.

"Yeah, right. And I'll have to pull an *Omarosa* on you!" Paris retorted.

"Neither one of you can fire the other," Naoko said, walking into the office. "What's all the shouting about?"

Milan and Paris exchanged dubious glances. "Oh, just a little sisterly rivalry," Milan answered.

"Well, for a moment I thought I was walking into THE APPRENTICE boardroom!" Naoko joked.

"Speaking of which, where were you this morning?" Milan questioned him.

He took his hand and smoothed it over his neatly trimmed head. "A man's gotta do what a man's gotta do!"

They all laughed.

"We missed your opinions at the Reality Ruckus," Paris added.

"Don't worry. *Opinions* are something I never lack!"

More laughter erupted.

Milan told them both that she had a call to make.

"I think she wants to get rid of us," Paris whispered to Naoko.

"No, I *really* have to make an important phone call," Milan said, responding to her sister's jest.

"Say no more," Naoko stated, throwing his hands up. "I actually need to speak privately with Paris anyway."

Milan glanced at her sister. Paris averted her eyes.

"All right then. I guess we won't keep you from your *important* call," Paris said, her tone condescending.

Milan simply fanned the air with her hand before shooing the two of them out of her office.

CHAPTER
THIRTY-THREE

Arriving back at her office Paris invited Naoko to have a seat. As he obliged, she couldn't help but notice how handsome he looked – sort of GQ-ish with his blue jeans, a pair of black designer slip-on shoes, white button-down shirt and a black blazer. She'd never looked at him in *that* way before. Her thoughts of him as someone more than an employee surprised her. She quickly dismissed them.

"So, what's on your mind?" she asked, settling into her own chair.

He suddenly had that nervous little boy look on his face again. "Uh, well. I won't take up much of your time, Paris. I just wanted to give you this," he said, reaching inside his blazer and retrieving a white envelope and then handing it across the desk to her.

"What's this, Naoko?"

"Open it."

With some apprehension creeping over her, Paris removed a letter-opener from her desk and ripped through the envelope. She removed the one-page letter and read it. Her eyes widened in surprise as her breath caught in her throat. "You're resigning!" she finally stated, which was more of an exclamation than a question.

He nodded. "I have no choice."

"What do you mean? Naoko, you cannot resign!"

He remained silent, choosing to stare at his hands as they

lay folded on his lap.

"Does this have anything to do with our conversation the other day?" Paris pressed him.

He looked up at her. "Paris, didn't you say that you don't date your employees?"

"Yes, but . . ."

"Well, that's a problem you no longer have to worry about," he interrupted her.

Paris gave an exasperated sigh. "Naoko, do you really believe that by you resigning, you and I will suddenly develop this magical relationship? C'mon! You're smarter than that!"

"Paris, what I believe is what you told me."

"What I told you is that I am your boss and you are my employee! And be that as it may, I said we could also be friends. But nothing romantic is going to happen between us, Naoko. I'm sorry."

He'd become angry. "Well, if *I'm* not the problem, as you also stated, then why won't you give me a chance?"

Paris couldn't believe how difficult he was making this whole situation. And if he didn't back off real soon she was inclined to accept this resignation. "Naoko, this is a conversation that you and I cannot continue. I'm not accepting your resignation. However, I suggest you rethink your decision over the weekend and if by Monday you feel the same way, then I will respect your decision." She stood from her desk to escort him from her office.

Reluctantly, he got up and headed towards the door. He stopped before exiting and turned to face her. "I'm sorry if I upset you, Paris. I didn't mean to."

She shrugged it off. "I'm not upset, Naoko. However, I do believe that some lines may have been crossed and I don't won't that to ever happen again."

He nodded before allowing his head to drop. As he left her office he asked if she'd mind if he took the rest of the day off. She told him that it was okay. And then, with his chin sunk dejectedly into his chest, Naoko disappeared down the corridor.

CHAPTER
THIRTY-FOUR

Roberto Mendoza had spent most of the Friday afternoon ransacking the basement of his Miami home trying to find an old telephone directory. He knew that if he found the small booklet he'd also find the telephone number for his sister's ex-husband in Atlanta. At least he assumed the man was an *ex-husband* by now.

Many years had passed since he'd received the phone call from his brother-in-the-law asking if he knew where his sister was. At the time, he hadn't spoken to Nicole in at least six years. The two of them never quite got along. Although he was ten years older than his sister, it held little to no significance. Nicole could be as stubborn as a mule. He had tried to convince her to finish college before jumping head first into modeling. But she didn't listen. After only one year she dropped out of college and signed with some New York modeling agency.

He never doubted that his sister was a very beautiful woman, but he'd heard many sad stories about young women entering the modeling industry without a solid education to fall back on. But trying to share those stories with his sister was like trying to stick a pencil through a brick. And her timing couldn't have been worse. Their mother was very sick at the time and it certainly would have made her life a little brighter to know that her daughter was going to graduate college.

His resentment of his sister began to build when she took

on some international assignments and began traveling around the world, leaving him alone to care for their ailing mother. Nicole wasn't even in the States at the time of their mother's passing. When she finally did return home, cutting short her assignments in Italy and France, she abruptly moved from Miami to Atlanta. A few weeks later, Roberto had received a wedding invitation in the mail announcing his sister's marriage to someone named Everson Alexander. Needless to say, he was furious with Nicole. He'd tried talking some sense into her over the telephone, but it became apparent to him that her mind had been made up. She never explained to him how she even met the guy. Yet she was quite adamant that she was in love. That telephone conversation would be the last one that he'd have with his sister for several years to come.

Roberto Mendoza still hasn't spoken to his sister. Almost two years ago, *August 22, 2002*, he received a birthday card from his sister. She'd also written a note saying that she was doing okay and how sorry she was for not keeping in touch, and that she hoped to one day mend fences with him. She didn't say where she was living, although the birthday card's envelope had an Atlanta postmark.

At the age of sixty-three now, Roberto had reached a point in his life where he wanted to reconcile with his sister. She was his only family. He realized now that he should have never allowed so much time to pass between them. There was so much that he didn't know about her, and she knew little to nothing about him, especially the fact that she was an aunt to two handsome nephews.

As he grabbed another box from the shelf in the basement, he dropped it on the floor and sat on top of it. His eyes began to well up. He reached into his back pocket and retrieved a handkerchief and wiped his eyes clear. He simply had to find Nicole. The thought of never seeing her again caused his heart to ache tremendously. It wasn't just a matter of wanting to catch up on old times or make amends for the way they'd treated one another. For him that was definitely water under the bridge. Two weeks ago Roberto was diagnosed with prostate cancer, which had already spread to other parts of his body. His future outlook was not good.

Finding his sister had now become a matter of life and death. And while he was painfully aware that finding the last telephone number that he had for her could prove futile, he realized that he had to start somewhere.

He'd called the New York modeling agency where she had worked, but they would only tell him that she hadn't work for them in over twenty-five years. So finding the telephone number for her last known husband was imperative.

Suddenly a horrendous thought occurred to him. What if his sister was no longer living? Something could have happened to her over the years and no one would have known how to reach him. Roberto quickly dismissed that morbid thought. Of course his sister was alive! He knew that she was out there – *somewhere*. And he had absolutely no intentions of leaving this life until he found her.

CHAPTER
THIRTY-FIVE

Norah Jones' very beautiful and soothing voice provided the background music as they sorted through items late Friday evening. Milan and Paris had decided to lend a hand to their aunt. Trying to decide which of their father's items to keep and which to give away was not such an easy thing to do.

"I agree with Aunt Millie," Paris said, taking a bite of the PAPA JOHN'S pizza that had been delivered minutes earlier. "We can just sell the furniture along with the house."

"Well, that's probably not a bad idea," agreed Milan. "Besides, I've always heard that a house filled with furniture is often easier to sell than an empty one."

Everson's clothes were being donated to the Salvation Army as well as to some local churches. Aunt Millie was sorting through Everson's personal papers. She never realized that her brother was such a pack rat. It appeared that he saved every letter and card that he'd received over the years. She found a card that she'd given him when he launched his advertising agency. And there were various handmade cards given by the twins when they were little.

"What are you smiling about?" Milan asked, glancing over at her aunt.

"Oh, I'm just reminiscing, that's all," Aunt Millie replied.

Milan returned a smile.

"What do you girls have planned for Valentine's Day tomorrow?" Aunt Millie asked them.

Milan was busying herself by thumbing through her father's CD collection so Paris answered. "Sydney is flying in later tonight and he and I are having dinner tomorrow evening at the SUNDIAL."

Aunt Millie didn't seem surprised. "Why don't that young man just *move* here?" she stated. "I mean he's been doing a lot of flying back and forth lately."

"Aunt Millie, Sydney is being prepared to assume control of his mother's ad agency, I don't think he'll be moving to Atlanta any time soon," Paris explained.

"Speaking of Sydney," Milan piped in. "Blade wanted me to ask you something, Sis."

"What's that?"

"Well, he along with others involved in this acquisition on our behalf, would very much like to meet with Mirabella Salinas prior to this deal closing. And, well, they have not had any success in scheduling a meeting with her so . . ."

"I guess he wants me to talk with Sydney about it," Paris interrupted.

"Well, you do seem to have the man's ear," Milan said.

"You know, I wondered about that myself," Aunt Millie began. "From what you girls have told me, this acquisition is supposed to happen within a couple of weeks and yet this *Mirabella* woman has yet to visit our offices."

"It makes you wonder if she's serious about the whole thing," Milan added.

"Of course she's serious!" Paris defended the unknown woman. "Why else would she allow her son to fly back and forth from Dallas to Atlanta to handle the deal?"

"Well, with all due respect, Sis, you can't really say that his trips have been all *business.*"

"I resent your insinuation, Milan."

"Well, it's true. I mean you two have been spending a lot of time together lately. I'm surprised he haven't invited *you* to Dallas to meet his mother."

Paris rolled her eyes at her sister. "You fail to understand that the woman is running a multi-million dollar ad agency, okay? I'm sure she doesn't have the time to be jetting all over the place unless it's really necessary. Besides, Sydney told me that she doesn't like to get involved in such deals until the "deal is actually ready to be finalized."

"Come look at this picture," Aunt Millie said, changing the subject. She held up a picture of the girls on their ninth birthday. "You girls haven't changed much at all," she said. Milan and Paris laughed when they saw the picture.

"I guess daddy never knew what to do with our hair," Milan said.

"Yeah, it was easier for him to just give us both ponytails," Paris said, chuckling.

As Aunt Millie dug deeper into the box of photos she came across several pictures of Nicole. They were obviously from her days of modeling. She wasn't sure if she should show them to the twins or not.

"What you got there, Aunt Millie?" Paris asked, attempting to peek over her aunt's shoulder.

Aunt Millie quickly tried to shield the photos beneath some other ones within the box.

"Are those pictures of our mom?" Paris asked, having caught a glance of the photos.

"Our mom?" Milan echoed.

Aunt Millie gave a deep sigh. "They're just some photos that your father kept of your mother when she worked as a model."

"A model?" the twins said simultaneously.

Their reaction caught Aunt Millie by surprise. "Your father never told you that your mom was a model?"

They shook their heads. "We rarely talked about her," Milan said. "Can we see the pictures?"

"Are you sure you girls want to do this?"

The twins exchanged nervous glances. "I'm okay with it," Paris stated. "I mean I'm just curious."

The twins could only recall the one time that their father had shown them pictures of their mother. It was when they were ten years of age and he'd decided to tell them that their mother hadn't died during childbirth, but that she had in fact abandoned them. Neither could even recall what their mother looked like because they only saw the handful of pictures once when they little girls.

Reluctantly, Aunt Millie handed the photos to Paris. Milan joined her sister on the sofa to look at them.

Both their eyes blinked with incredulity when they saw the first photo. "Was our mom *Italian* or something?" Milan asked, noticing their mother's smooth bronze beige complexion.

"She is so beautiful," Paris remarked, allowing her fingers to glide over the photo. "Her face looks like one of those porcelain dolls."

"Your mother isn't Italian," Aunt Millie answered. "I believe your father said that she was from Cuba or Spain. I can't remember."

"She looks like *Penelope Cruz*," Milan said.

"No, I think she looks more like *Salma Hayek!*" Paris interjected.

Aunt Millie laughed. "Listen to you two. She looks like your mother."

"Well, it's looks like we got our hair from her and our skin tone from daddy," Milan said.

"Yeah, that's definitely the case," Paris agreed.

The twins continued to browse at the other photos. "Why did she leave us?" Paris asked, to no one in particular. Her eyes brimmed with tears. And as on cue, Milan's eyes became filled as well.

"Girls," Aunt Millie began. "Don't do this to yourselves."

"But there are so many unanswered questions!" Paris shouted. "Why didn't she love us? How could she just abandon us? Was she ashamed of us?"

"Paris, *please*. I don't think that it had anything whatsoever to do with you girls. Something terrible must have happened in your mother's life to cause her to do what she did. You girls, nor your father, are to blame."

"I guess we'll never know," Milan added.

Paris dried her eyes with the back of her hand. "I wonder if she even thinks about us?"

"Oh, I'm sure she hasn't forgot about you," Aunt Millie assured them.

"Aunt Millie, did you spend a lot of time with her?" Milan asked.

"Well, I can't say that I spent a whole lot of time with your mother. I mean everything sort of happened quickly. Everson told me that he met your mother at a business event, and apparently they must have clicked right away because before "long Everson was telling me that they were getting married."

The telephone rang, startling the twins. "I thought the phone service had been disconnected?" Paris stated.

Aunt Millie shook her head. "No, I didn't want to do that until the house actually went on the market."

Milan went over to answer the phone that was setting on a nearby end table. "Hello," she answered.

The person on the other end cleared his throat excessively. "Uh, I not sure if I have correct number, but I need to speak with *Everson Alexander.*"

Milan's breath caught in her throat. She didn't recognize the thick accent of the male voice on the other end. "Who is this?" she demanded.

"My name is *Roberto. Roberto Mendoza.*"

"How do you know my father?"

Paris and Aunt Millie immediately gave their attention to Milan.

"He married once to my sister."

Slowly, the telephone dropped from Milan's hand as she stood with her face void of expression. Aunt Millie raced to the phone. "Hello! Who is this?" she spoke rapidly.

Paris guided her sister back to the sofa. "Milan, who's on the phone?"

Milan took a deep breath. "I think it's our *uncle.*"

The twins listened intently as their Aunt Millie spoke into the telephone. "My brother died a year and a half ago," they heard her say. "As far as I know he had no communication with Nicole since he last phoned you about her."

Aunt Millie began to explain to him what's happened over the past few years. "No, I haven't seen or spoken to your sister either," she told the caller. Then there was a brief moment of silence. The twins watched as their aunt's face became tight, pinched. "I'm so sorry to hear that," she stated, her voice low and etched with concern. She motioned for one of the girls to get her something to write on. Paris quickly retrieved a piece of paper from the kitchen counter and handed it to her aunt.

"Okay, I'm ready," Aunt Millie said. She took down the telephone number that he gave her. She assured him that if she happened to hear anything from Nicole that she would be certain to give him a call. He apologized for disturbing them and thanked her for any assistance that she might be able to provide in helping to locate his sister.

"Was that really our mom's brother?" Milan asked, after Aunt Millie hung up the telephone.

"I'm afraid so."

"Why was he asking for daddy?" Paris asked.

Aunt Millie sat back on the sofa next to the twins. "Well, his name is Roberto. He lives in Miami. He's your mother's only brother. Now, I've never met him before, but I do remember Everson trying to reach him when your mother disappeared. Unfortunately, when your dad finally reached him he hadn't seen or heard from your mother in over six years."

"Six years?" the twins said, surprised.

"Apparently they were estranged. Anyway, he asked your father not to bother him anymore. And as far as I know, your father never called again after that."

"Why is he calling now?" Paris asked.

Aunt Millie lowered her head. "He's dying from prostate cancer."

"Oh my god!" Milan gasped.

Aunt Millie went on to share with the twins what Roberto had explained to her over the phone. The twins couldn't believe that they had an uncle whom they'd never even met. The whole situation made them wonder just what kind of person Nicole was – abandoning her husband, her babies *and* her brother.

Their conversation on the matter would continue for another hour before Paris announced that she had to drive to the airport to pick up Sydney. Milan decided to head home as well. Aunt Millie thanked them both for coming over to help out. She told them that she was going to hang around the house for a little while longer.

After the twins were gone, Aunt Millie pulled off the top from a shoebox that she'd came across right before the twins had arrived. She didn't want them to see it so she had hidden the shoebox behind the bookcase. Now she had a chance to examine the document inside the shoebox carefully. As she looked over the document again her mind began racing. Was it really *possible*? It didn't make any sense. She knew that the document itself was real. But she wanted to be absolutely certain.

Aunt Millie picked up the telephone and dialed the number that she'd written on the piece of paper earlier. After several rings Roberto finally answered.

"Hello, Mister Mendoza. It's Mildred Alexander in Atlanta."

"Señorita Alexander! You have information for me?"

"Actually, no. But I'd like to ask you a question that, depending on the answer, might be helpful in locating your sister."

Roberto was all ears.

CHAPTER
THIRTY-SIX

"**Thanks** for making this Valentine's Day very special for me," Paris told Sydney as she drove him back to his hotel late Saturday night.

"I owe you the thanks," he replied. "I don't believe that I've ever had such an enjoyable dinner."

Paris smiled at him coquettishly.

"I'm serious, Paris. You always seem to make me feel so incredible whenever we're together."

She reached over and squeezed his hand. "That goes ditto for me."

There was a moment of silence in the car.

"Sydney," Paris began. "I need to ask you something."

"Of course. You can ask me anything that you wish, personal or otherwise."

"Well, unfortunately it's business."

"It must really be important if you're addressing it tonight?"

"No, not really. I just don't want to forget. The thing is . . . well, you've met our attorney, Blade Barnes, right?"

Sydney nodded.

"Well, he asked Milan if I'd speak to you about trying to get a meeting scheduled with your mother."

Sydney ran his fingers through his hair. "I see. Everyone wants to meet the great, powerful *Mirabella Salinas!*"

Paris chuckled. "Now you've piqued my interest!"

"Oh, like you haven't been interested at all in meeting my

"mother!" he joked.

"Yeah, I'd like to meet her, but I wouldn't say that I'm anxious. And I don't think Blade is either. I mean they just find it strange that your agency is buying our agency and yet we've never met the owner of your agency."

"I know. I was only kidding. Actually, I've been trying to get my mother to accompany me here but she insists on waiting until the deal is ready to close."

"That's what I explained to Milan. I mean I'm sure she's a very busy woman."

Sydney nodded. "Yes, she keeps a full plate. But hey, when you do meet her I know that you will love her."

Paris flashed him a knowing smile. "Well, I love her *son* don't I?"

"And her son loves you!" Sydney leaned over the armrest and gave her a kiss on the cheek.

Paris turned into the hotel's parking lot and parked at the front entrance.

"Do you want to come up?" he asked.

Paris looked at her watch. It was nearing midnight. "Thanks, but it's getting late. I'll take a rain check."

He displayed a wounded expression on his face. "Well, I guess I'm going to have to change my plans."

"What are you talking about?"

"Shh," he said, placing a finger to her lips. "If you don't mind, can we at least park some place other than the front door?"

Paris raised one eyebrow in a questioning slant. "What are you up to, Mister Salinas?"

"Just move the car over there," he said, pointing to a space across the parking lot.

She eyed him skeptically before driving the car from the front entrance and parking it in one of the parking spaces. "What else will you have me do, Mister Salinas?"

"I'm glad you asked," he answered. "First, I want you to close your eyes."

Paris gave him a critical squint before finally closing her eyes. Less than ten seconds later he asked her to open them again. Sitting in the palm of his hand was a small TIFFANY box. Her heart began to soar as her eyes became moist with joy. And as Sydney began to lift the top from the box her anticipation grew.

"*This* is why I wanted you to come up," he said, removing the top off the box. He opened the ring box and held the diamond before her eyes. Although it was dark inside the car, the moon gave off a shimmer of light shining through the windshield.

Paris clasped her hand over her mouth as she stared at the two-carat marquise diamond ring.

"From the first day that I saw you, Paris Alexander, I knew in my heart that you where meant for me. I know that we have not known each other very long, but I also know that I am in love with you and that I want to love you every day of my life. So, before the clock strikes midnight, on this February fourteenth, two-thousand-four, I am asking if you will marry me?"

By now her face was drenched in tears. Yet the brilliance of the diamond continued to shine before her. She was speechless. She knew that Sydney could be full of surprises, but she never expected this.

Gazing candidly at him she finally spoke. "Sydney, I don't know what to say. I mean you have totally caught me by surprise!"

"I know. And I don't mean to put you on the spot, but Paris I want you in my life. Right now, marrying you is the only thing I want in this world – well, other than *world peace* and *good will* toward all men."

She laughed. "You are so silly!"

"Yes, I'm *silly* in love! So, don't keep me in suspense, my Valentine. Will you marry me?"

CHAPTER
THIRTY-SEVEN

With rain drizzle still clinging to her umbrella as she made her way down the corridor, Milan shivered from the cool wet weather outside. The entire office floor had been dark and quiet when she'd arrived. Flipping on the main light switches behind the receptionist's desk quickly illuminated the early Monday morning. She realized that she was the first person to arrive. It was just shy of six o'clock.

Milan wanted to get a jump on the week. She had three meetings scheduled for later today and the paperwork on her desk was about to form a mutiny.

Reaching her office she noticed a piece of paper taped to Paris' door. Setting down her attaché case and umbrella, Milan removed the paper. It was a standard size sheet of paper, which had been tri-folded. Without hesitation she unfolded the *note*, which clearly had her *sister's* name written on the outside. Milan read the handwritten note anyway.

> DEAR PARIS, I TOOK SOME TIME TO THINK ABOUT MY DECISION LIKE WE DISCUSSED AND I'M SORRY TO SAY THAT I HAVE NO CHOICE BUT TO RESIGN MY POSITION AT THE AGENCY. I JUST DON'T THINK THAT I CAN CONTINUE TO WORK HERE KNOWING HOW I FEEL ABOUT YOU, AND I DON'T WANT TO MAKE THINGS AWKWARD FOR YOU. I WILL COME LATER THIS WEEK TO CLEAR OUT MY OFFICE. AGAIN, I'M VERY SORRY. NAOKO – J.R.I.L.Y.

Milan was surprised after reading the note. The agency could not afford to lose Naoko right now. But she was even more surprised by what her sister has apparently been keeping from her. She decided to keep the note and confront her sister when she got in. Gathering up her things she unlocked her door and stepped into her office. She removed her jacket and placed it on the hook behind her door. The umbrella was dropped on the floor behind the door as well. Since she was the first to arrive she'd have to get the coffee started. It was one of their little rules around the office. After putting away her purse and attaché case, Milan was about to head towards the break room when her telephone began ringing. She glanced at her watch – it wasn't even six-fifteen – who could be calling her this early? She decided to allow the call to go into her voice-mail.

When she returned from the break room Milan picked up the telephone and punched in the code for the voice-mailbox. The call was from her Aunt Millie saying that she wasn't feeling well today and would not be in the office. A couple of coughs had been added for good measure. Aunt Millie told her that there would be no need to call and check on her because she was going to rest most of the day.

Hanging up the phone, Milan thought the call had been strange. Aunt Millie seemed fine on Friday when she and Paris were over to the house. And why would she call so early in the morning? To her office? Aunt Millie would usually call either her or Paris at home regarding something like this. It almost seemed as if she wanted to get the voice-mail because she knew that she didn't generally get into the office until nine o'clock, except for their Friday mornings' *Reality Ruckus.*

Milan considered calling her aunt back but quickly decided against it. Although Aunt Millie's behavior was indicative of employees who were job-interviewing behind their employer's back, she hoped that wasn't the case. The agency had been very fortunate not to lose any employees in the wake of their financial crisis. Which, of course, was why she planned to have a serious talk with Paris about Naoko's impending departure. She'd told her sister that the man was crazy about her, but she wouldn't take it seriously. Milan read the note again. Apparently the two of them *have* been discussing the situation, she realized. Paris must have given him her speech about not dating people she worked with. Milan hoped that her sister had let the man down easy.

A thought occurred to her. If Sydney's agency acquires theirs, then her sister will be working with *him*. And with her obvious love for Sydney Salinas, Milan wondered how her sister was going to deal with that? Oh well. That was Paris' bridge to cross, not hers.

CHAPTER
THIRTY-EIGHT

The 7:35 A.M. flight had taken off on time. With rain still falling at the airport, Aunt Millie was certain that her flight would be delayed. But it had been cleared for takeoff as scheduled.

As the jet continued to gain altitude, she closed her eyes and began to prepare herself for what she was about to encounter. Lying to Milan disturbed her greatly. But it had to be done – at least for now.

A leather portfolio lay on her lap. She opened it and stared at the document again, studying it acutely. There simply had to be some connection, she thought. If her intuition turned out to be wrong then so be it. The girls would not have to know.

Her mind drifted more on the twins. Those girls would always be very special and dear to her heart. They've endured so much in their young lives. She would not allow anyone to harm them. Aunt Millie recalled last summer's incident at the office with that Raleigh Robinson. The entire fiasco was a nightmare. Had she been there wild horses couldn't have prevented her from attacking that crazy man and beating the devil out of him with her bare hands! Gun or not. Yet, the girls had dealt with the incident with remarkable resolve. It amazed her at times how the two of them seem to draw strength from one another at just the right moment. Milan had certainly helped Paris cope with the revelation last month that her baby's father was partly to blame for their father's death. Even she hadn't quite gotten over that yet.

For a moment she second-guessed her decision to make this trip. Perhaps she should just leave well enough alone. The girls had enough to deal with just running the ad agency. They didn't need any more surprises.

Aunt Millie quickly realized, however, that the trip was inevitable. There was absolutely no way that she was going to simply sit around waiting for the other shoe to drop.

The captain's voice suddenly infiltrated the cabin announcing to the passengers that the plane had reached its cruising altitude and that they were now free to move about the cabin. Immediately the unlocking of seatbelts could be heard throughout the coach section. Aunt Millie's seatbelt remained secured around her waist. She wasn't about to go *roaming* around the cabin. She'd heard stories of passengers being thrown wildly about because an airplane hit an unexpected air pocket. Her bottom would be glued to her seat until the plane landed at its destination.

Aunt Millie adjusted her seat from its upright position. She took notice of the time on her watch. Okay – within two hours she'd be there. For now, she'd relax and enjoy this tranquil view from thirty-five thousand feet.

CHAPTER
THIRTY-NINE

"**Good** morning! Thank you for calling the ALEXANDER AGENCY. How may I direct your call?" Belinda knew that she'd have her hands full. The switchboard on Monday mornings always seemed to be jammed. "I'm sorry, but Naoko Jackson isn't answering – would you like his voice-mail?" She couldn't understand why Naoko hadn't arrived at the office yet. He was rarely late, she thought as she checked the time. It was 8:47. Belinda decided to buzz Paris' office to see if Naoko was planning on coming in today. Just as she prepared to do so Paris stepped from the elevators.

"Hey, Belinda," she greeted. "How was your weekend?"

"Hi Paris. I had a great weekend! And you?"

"Wonderful!" Paris answered as she continued her quick stroll past Belinda's desk.

"Paris, wait!" Belinda called out.

She turned around and trekked back towards the lobby. "What Is it, Belinda?"

"I just wanted to know if you know whether or not Naoko will be in? He's been getting a lot of calls and I haven't heard from him this morning."

Paris was clad in designer boots, a mini fur, and matching hat, scarf and gloves. She unraveled the scarf from around her neck and threw it over her shoulder. "Uh, let me find out and I'll let you know, okay?"

"Sure."

When Paris arrived at her office the door was partially opened. She stepped inside and found her sister sitting at her desk. "Hey, girl."

"Good morning, Sis. You're a little late aren't you?"

Paris began removing her coat, hat and scarf and placing them on the hook behind her door. "Yeah, I know. I had a crazy weekend."

"I guess so. I tried calling you several times yesterday."

Paris walked over to her desk and motioned for her sister to move out of her chair. Milan took a seat across from her desk. "I took Tristan and Nikki to brunch, and then I took Tristan shopping. Later, we stopped by one of his friend's house so he could play awhile and I got to talking with the boy's mother, which was a mistake because the woman didn't know when to shut up and . . ."

"I called your cell phone too," Milan interrupted.

Paris let out a sigh. "I turned it off earlier and forgot to turn it back on."

Milan stared at her sister incredulously.

"Okay, don't believe me then!" Paris said, correctly reading her sister's face.

"This is *me* you're talking to, Sis. Now, if you spent a long weekend with Sydney, just go ahead and admit it!" Milan teased.

"Sydney and I had dinner on Saturday just like we planned *and* just like I told you we were going to."

"Just dinner?"

Paris rolled her eyes. "Don't even go there, girl."

Milan watched as her sister began shuffling papers, pretending to be straightening her desk. She noticed her sister's clad hands. "What's with the gloves?"

"My hands are still cold," Paris answered nonchalantly.

"Cold? Paris, it is not cold in here!"

"That's because you've obviously had time to warm up. I just came from outside, where it's raining and thirty-something degrees, okay?"

"Oh, please!" Without warning, Milan reached over the desk and grabbed one of her sister's arms and began pulling off the glove.

"Hey! Stop, Milan!" Paris shouted.

Milan ignored her sister's plea. By now her entire body was stretched across the desk as he continued to loosen Paris' fingers from the glove. In between laughter and screams for her sister to *quit*, Paris could hardly put up much resistance. Finally, Milan had succeeded and getting the glove off.

"Whoa!" she said, her eyes locking onto the shiny diamond ring.

Paris yanked her hand from her sister's grasp. "Satisfied?"

"Tell me that is not what I think it is, Paris?"

Paris turned up her nose to her sister as she took off her other glove and stuffed both into her desk drawer.

"Sis, no more playing, all right? Is that an engagement ring?"

Paris held up her hand in front of her eyes and began admiring the precious jewel. "I haven't decided yet."

"Are you crazy! I mean you and Sydney have only known each other for less than two months!"

"And what does that have to do with anything?"

"A lot!"

"Milan, you know how I feel about Sydney. I think he's the one."

Milan was desperately fighting back tears. "Paris, don't. Please. Give yourself time. I mean can't you see how fast things are moving? The man is buying our agency, you don't know what impact that could have on your relationship."

"His *mother* is buying our agency," Paris corrected her sister.

Milan fanned the air with her hand. "There's no difference! He is being groomed to take over *her* agency."

"I am twenty-six years old, Milan. I think that I am capable of choosing what I want for my life."

Milan tilted her head back and exhaled towards the ceiling. "I hear what you're saying, Sis. I just want you to be sure, that's all."

"Which is why I haven't given him an answer yet."

"And he gave you the ring anyway?"

"Yeah. I think he thinks that by me wearing it I'll be more likely to say *yes*."

Milan leaned over her sister's desk. "Let me see that rock," she said, grabbing Paris' hand. "It is gorgeous," Milan remarked. "The man has good taste."

"Of course," Paris stated. "He assured me that he covered the four C's when he selected it," she added, referring to the diamond's *cut, color, clarity* and *carat.*

"Well, to be honest, I think that you two make a great couple. Just don't rush anything."

"You know me better than that, Milan. Besides, even if I were to tell him 'yes' today, it's not like we would be getting married tomorrow! That would be at least a year away."

"Well, that's good to know."

Paris' phone began ringing. "Excuse me, Milan," she told her sister as she picked up the receiver. "This is Paris."

It was Belinda wanting to know if their Aunt Millie was coming in today.

"I thought she was already in," Paris answered her. "Um, hold on a minute." She cupped her hand over the telephone's mouthpiece. "Hey, Milan. Do you know if Aunt Millie is coming in? Belinda needs to know."

"Oh, she left me a voice-mail this morning saying that she didn't feel well," Milan answered.

"So is she coming in?"

Milan shook her head. "She said she would be resting at home today."

"Okay. Belinda, she's out ill today," Paris said into the phone. Then Belinda wanted to know the status of Naoko. "Um, I haven't had a chance to check on that, but I'll do it right away and let you know. Okay. Thanks." She hung up the phone.

"Sis, when were you going to tell me about Naoko?"

"What do you mean?" Paris responded, obviously playing dumb about the matter.

Milan grabbed the note that she'd stuck between some envelopes on her sister's desk and handed it to her. "It was taped to your door this morning."

Paris looked at the front of the note and saw her name written on it. "Oh, and I guess the fact that it has *my name* all over it and that it was taped to *my door*, didn't dawn upon you that it was for *my eyes* only?"

Milan shrugged her shoulders.

Paris gave her sister the eye roll again before reading the note. "I'm handling the situation," she uttered, folding the note and placing it aside.

"Sis, we can't afford to lose someone like him."

"I'm aware of that, Milan. But I'm not going to start dating the man just to keep him at the agency."

"How do you know that's what he wants?"

"Trust me, I know."

"So, it was him who sent those flowers last week, wasn't it?"

"That won't be happening again."

"Is that why he's resigning?"

"No. Well, sort of. I mean I told Naoko that I don't date people I work with and . . ."

"You sure about that?" Milan interrupted. "Technically speaking, Sydney will soon be someone you're working with."

"That's different."

"Really?"

"Milan, stop trying to confuse me! Now you've made me lose my train of thought!"

"Just pointing out the obvious."

"Oh, now I remember. Okay, what I was explaining to you, before being rudely interrupted, is that Naoko has the idea that if we didn't work together that maybe I'll consider a relationship with him. That's why he's thinking about resigning."

"Thinking about it? According to that note, Sis, he done done it!"

"Well, I'll just have to talk him out of it."

There was a loud knock at her door. "Come in," Paris answered. It was one of their account executives. The young woman looked as if all the blood had drained from her face.

"Charla, is something wrong?" Milan spoke first.

"Channel forty-six just showed a *breaking news* bit on the television in the break room," she began. "There's been an accident."

"What kind of an accident?" Milan asked, nervously.

The young woman hesitated, and then turning her eyes towards Paris she answered, "Where does your son catch his school bus?"

Paris' face immediately grew flush. "Oh my god! What's happened!"

Being careful to choose her words Charla answered, "Well, a semi-tractor smashed into a school bus at the intersection of Holcomb Bridge Road and Georgia 400."

Both sisters clasped their hand over their mouth.

"Could you see the name on the school bus?" Milan asked her.

Charla took a deep breath; tears were already forming in her eyes. "It was a THORNHILL CHRISTIAN ACADEMY bus."

Paris sprung from her chair. "I got to get over there!"

"Paris, wait!" Charla shouted. "They said that all of the kids were injured. Some of them have already been transported to different hospitals."

"What do you mean, *some*?" Milan yelled.

Charla burst into tears. Her reaction opened the floodgates for tears to begin streaming from Milan and Paris as well. "There . . . there were . . . some fatalities!" she sobbed.

Paris suddenly felt weak in the knees. The air was collapsing around her. Milan could see that her sister looked incredibly faint. She rushed over to her side. "I'll drive you, Paris."

As the three of them tore from the building, Charla began dialing on her cell phone. *North Fulton Regional Hospital* was closest to the scene of the accident so she called there first. Some students had been brought there but the hospital didn't have a list of names yet. Since their office was less than a mile away from *Northside Hospital*, Milan decided to take a chance and drive over there first.

Several news vehicles were arriving at the hospital at the same time as Milan sped into the parking lot. She drove directly to the emergency room entrance and parked her car in an illegal spot. They all bolted from the car, the wind blowing cold rain into their faces, mixing bitterly alongside their anxious tears.

CHAPTER
FORTY

Riding in the back of the taxi was anything but smooth for Aunt Millie. Leaving the airport the taxi driver drove like *he* was late for an appointment. And now as they headed towards downtown he was weaving in and out of lanes like a racecar driver. She couldn't wait until he got her to her destination. Her stomach was all tied up in knots at the moment.

Finally, the taxi came to a stop in front of the glistening skyscraper. Aunt Millie reached inside her purse and pulled out a few bills to pay the fare. She considered not tipping him, but did so anyway. There was no luggage to retrieve from the trunk of the taxi, since this was only going to be a one-day trip, so Aunt Millie quickly exited the taxi. No sooner had she closed the door the taxi driver peeled from the curb, tires squealing like a bunch of angry pigs. Maybe he gets a commission on the *total number* of passengers he picks up, she thought to herself, shaking her head and watching the yellow vehicle disappear into traffic.

Aunt Millie retrieved from her purse the piece of paper that she'd written down the address. She had the correct building. Standing in front the building she attempted to look upwards at the structure but the glare of the sun altered her vision.

She glanced at her watch. It showed 10:30. But she was now in the central time zone so it was only 9:30 here. *Let's get this over with*, she whispered, walking inside the building.

CHAPTER
FORTY-ONE

SALINAS WORLDWIDE occupied three floors within the class-A office building. There were a total of sixty-seven floors inside the downtown skyscraper. SALINAS WORLDWIDE leased floors twenty-three, twenty-four and twenty-five.

Visitors to the advertising agency would first land on the twenty-third floor, where two receptionists seated behind a huge receptionist center that's constructed of limestone greet them. Azure lighting lurked from the ceiling like an ethereal sky, basking both visitors and employees in warmth and tranquility.

Aunt Millie had already announced herself to one of the receptionists. She told the young Latino woman that she needed to see Mirabella Salinas. And after a brief moment of interrogation about whether or not she had an *appointment*, Aunt Millie finally implored the young woman to phone Mirabella's office and inform her that she was from the ALEXANDER AGENCY in Atlanta and that it was of the utmost importance that she see her immediately. Of course, the receptionist was quite aware of their pending acquisition of the ALEXANDER AGENCY, so assuming that Aunt Millie was one of the agency's principals, she quickly phoned Mirabella's secretary. Minutes later another Latino woman descended the limestone staircase and led Aunt Millie up the stairs and to a VIP waiting area.

Aunt Millie sat quietly and patiently, admiring the agency's elegant offices. There was a stark contrast between their agency and this one. While the racial make-up of their agency was predominantly African-American, this one appeared to employ mostly Latinos. Aunt Millie became excited about all of the possibilities when the two agencies became one. At first she was skeptical about the whole thing, but over the past several weeks she realized that her brother would probably have done the same thing as the girls were doing if in fact he was presented with the same financial crisis.

Aunt Millie's thoughts were interrupted when Mirabella's secretary walked over. "Miss Salinas will see you now," she told her, as she escorted Aunt Millie past her desk and to the inner sanctum of this agency's chairwoman, president and CEO.

CHAPTER
FORTY-TWO

Northside Hospital did not have any of the children from the school bus accident. The person at the emergency room station directed them to *Scottish Rite*, which was just across the street. Milan, Paris and Charla rushed over there, all the while trying to keep their emotions in check. Scores of other anxious parents were also crowding the waiting area in the emergency room when they arrived. They were told that Tristan had been brought there and that his injuries were minor. The news brought a sigh of relief to all three of them. Paris threw her arms around her sister and sobbed, thanking God between her tears and sniffles.

A representative from THORNHILL CHRISTIAN ACADEMY had been dispatched to both hospitals where the children had been taken. Apparently the TV media, in their haste to get the news out quickly, had relied upon an unreliable source when they reported that there had been some fatalities. Actually, there were none. Although two of the students on the bus suffered serious injuries, they were not life threatening. Most of the children, including Tristan, were shaken by the accident. But any injuries sustained by the children were mainly small cuts and bruises.

An hour later Tristan had been given a clean bill of health. When Paris retrieved him from one of the rooms he looked quite scared. He was delighted to see her when she appeared in the room. A single BAND-AID graced his tiny forehead. And his eyes were still moist from where he'd been crying. The doctor told her that Tristan had checked out fine. The bandage was to cover a very small cut on his forehead that he'd apparently received from bumping it against one of the bus seats. Paris thanked the doctor.

When she arrived back to the waiting area, Nikki had arrived also. Tristan ran to greet her.

"Guess what, Nikki?" he shouted, obviously anxious to share his ordeal.

"Hey, big guy!" Nikki said, lifting him into her arms. "I'm so glad that you're okay."

"Uh-huh," Tristan said. "But guess what?"

"What, honey?"

"I got hit by a big truck!"

"You did!"

He nodded. "Uh-huh. And it didn't even hurt!"

Nikki gave him a hug. "Well, that's because you're such a strong little man!"

"No! Strong *big* man!"

Everyone laughed.

The representative came over and spoke briefly with them. He told them that he was happy to see that Tristan was doing well. He told Paris that a counselor would be available at the school tomorrow to help any of the students who needed to talk about the accident. Paris nodded. But at the moment she wasn't so sure if she wanted her son to return to THORNHILL CHRISTIAN ACADEMY. She realized that the bus incident was certainly an accident, but the entire school year had been laden with one thing after another. And now she was beginning to wonder if this was her cue to place her child in some other environment.

After the school representative had left them to speak with some other parents nearby, Nikki asked Paris if she wanted her to take Tristan home. Paris, however, feeling the need to remain near her son at the moment, decided that she would take Tristan to lunch and then let him stay at the office with her for the remainder of the day.

She gave Nikki a hug and thanked her for coming to the hospital. Milan picked up Tristan and carried him to the parking lot. She, too, was glad that her nephew was going to be all right. It was sad enough that Tristan would grow up without the presence of his father; Milan could not bear the thought of something terrible happening to him. Her sister's world would be devastated beyond repair.

"So, did you get hold of Aunt Millie?" Paris asked as the four of them made their way to Milan's car.

"No. I called the house several times and the answering machine kept picking up."

"Did you try her cell?"

Milan shook her head. "I didn't see the point because her message to me said that she was going to rest today, so I assumed that maybe she was asleep and had turned the ringer off."

"Yeah, you're probably right. Tristan and I will stop by her house on the way home this evening," Paris said.

As Tristan bounced along in his Aunt's arms he looked at the other woman walking alongside them. "What's your name?" he asked her.

"Charla, " she answered, smiling.

Feeling her arms about to give out, Milan put Tristan down to walk the rest of the way to the parking garage. When they first arrived at the hospital she parked in front of the Emergency Room entrance, just as she had done at the other hospital. But she later moved her car to the parking garage that was adjacent to the hospital.

"I was wondering how long you were planning to carry him," Paris remarked.

"Well, if he wasn't almost as tall as me I would have carried him all the way."

"You guys are lucky to be so tiny," Charla told them. "BALLYS is making a fortune off me!"

"Humph. We're not *that* tiny," Paris said.

"That's true. We've encountered and endured a lot of stress over the past year – that's what's been keeping our weight off," Milan added.

"Stress? That's how I've been gaining all mine!"

The three women laughed. Unwilling to be left out, Tristan began laughing as well, though he had no idea why.

CHAPTER
FORTY-THREE

"**Hello,** Mildred. It's been long time," Mirabella greeted her as Aunt Millie entered her spacious posh office.

A plethora of thoughts were racing through Aunt Millie's mind. She gave her the once-over. "Hello, Nicole."

Mirabella invited her to have a seat on her Italian leather sofa that was positioned in the sitting area of her office. Aunt Millie obliged.

"You must have million questions for me," Mirabella stated, taking a seat in a chair opposite the sofa.

Aunt Millie forced a laugh. "You can't begin to know what's going through my mind right now."

Mirabella threw a lock of hair over her shoulder. "So, how did you know it was *me*?"

"I didn't. I mean I wasn't looking for you. My brother and I gave up that search three years after you left him. But ever since you announced your intention to acquire our agency you have been the subject of several news articles. And there was a story about you in ADWEEK magazine a couple of weeks ago that caught my eye."

Mirabella nodded. "Yes, the one where they ran picture of me from my modeling."

"Well, they showed a then and now photo, and while it did catch my eye for a moment, I didn't really think too much about it because of the name, *Mirabella*. I've only known you as *Nicole*."

"*Nicole* is my middle name. When I was little girl it is the name my brother would use. He not like *Mirabella*."

Aunt Millie wondered if now would be the time to tell her about Roberto? But there were too many other issues that needed to be addressed. Besides, she didn't tell Nicole's brother that she would reveal his condition to his sister, but that she would let him know if she heard anything from her. Perhaps that was what she'd do. When she left Dallas she'd phone Roberto and let him know how to reach his sister.

"Well, I was going through some of Everson's belongings over the weekend and I came across your marriage license," Aunt Millie began to explain. "And when I saw your name listed as first initial *M* and then *Nicole Mendoza*, well, that is when I began thinking."

"How did you know *M* was for *Mirabella*?"

"Actually, I didn't. But I had a hunch and so I decided to call your bro . . ." Aunt Millie stopped her sentence. But it was too late, enough had already been said.

"My brother?"

She realized now that she had to say something. "Listen, Nicole. There is a lot going on right now. And I have to tell you that my main concern is the protection of my nieces. You have no idea of what they've been through lately."

"You talk to my brother?" she asked, not hearing anything else Aunt Millie had just uttered.

Aunt Millie exhaled strongly. "It was your brother who called me. Well, actually he was looking for Everson with the intent of finding you. I must say that I was surprised to learn that he had no idea that my brother had been killed because he hadn't spoken to you in years."

"My brother and I have differences. We not able to work things out."

"I don't know, Nicole. I mean you seem to have this pattern of abandoning family."

"I not abandon my brother!" she shouted. "He not want me to marry Everson."

"Be that as it may, you did abandon Everson as well as Milan and Paris!"

She looked away from Aunt Millie's glaring eyes.

"Why, Nicole? What possible reason could you have had

"for leaving your husband and newborn babies? What in the world were you thinking?"

Mirabella could feel all of her old memories surfacing again. Memories that were full of guilt, shame and hurt. There had been a time in her life where she thought that she had dealt with her past. She began to second-guess her decision to buy the ad agency. In the days and weeks prior to her decision to pursue the acquisition, she ignored the risks that she might face if she chose to try and acquire the ALEXANDER AGENCY. But she really wanted to help the girls out of a bind – her girls. Now, the Pandora's box had been opened.

"Mildred, I was very young woman. I didn't know what my life was becoming. Everything moved so fast. I drop out of college one day; I'm traveling to Italy the next. And then my mother passed away when I still out of country. How do young woman deal with that?"

Aunt Millie could see the tears forming in Nicole's eyes. "Those things happened before you met my brother. Why did you choose to marry him if you felt that you were not ready?"

Mirabella stood and walked over to her desk and retrieved some Kleenex tissues and began drying her eyes as she returned to her seat. "Your brother fall in love with me."

"So, what are you saying, Nicole? That you were not in love with my brother? Because that would be a very good reason not to marry him!"

"No! I not say that! I loved Everson and I still love my daughters!"

Aunt Millie had to utilize all the strength that she could muster to keep from ringing her former sister-in-law's neck. "Do you know how weak and pathetic you sound? You were married to my brother for two years before you split! And your twin daughters were only six months old!"

"You not think I feel bad, Mildred? For twenty-seven years I feel bad! You not know my pain inside of me! I not perfect wife! I not perfect mother! Maybe you have skeletons in your closet too!"

Aunt Millie laughed mockingly. "Nicole, believe me I understand that everyone has a skeleton or two in their closet, but we're talking about an entire darn cemetery!"

Mirabella dried her eyes some more. "You not understand. You angry right now."

"Angry? You tell me, Nicole? I mean you desert my brother; you abandon your daughters, and now twenty-seven years later you want to try and make it up to them by saving their father's agency? Suddenly you're their White Knight!"

"I not see it that way, Mildred. I have followed Everson's success for many years. I proud of his accomplishments. I not want to see his ad agency fail."

"Well, the girls could have considered other options."

"I know Milan and Paris work very hard to learn business and make business grow. I proud of them as well. This I do from my heart, Mildred. I not try to correct mistakes made in past. But future don't have to be mistake."

"So, all these years you've been keeping up with my brother's success and not once did you even consider picking up the telephone to call him? Let him know that you were all right? Let him know that you were not floating at the bottom of some river?" Aunt Millie could no longer restrain her emotions. Tears erupted from her like a volcano spewing hot lava.

Nearly speechless, Mirabella said, "I so sorry for all the pain I have caused."

"Everson loved you dearly, Nicole. You meant the world to him." Aunt Millie allowed her face to drop into her hands. The tears flowed faster and more intensely.

Mirabella retrieved more tissues from her desk and handed them to Aunt Millie. She then buzzed her secretary and asked her to bring in some hot tea. Minutes later a silver tray was brought in. It held a small porcelain teapot and two matching cups and saucers. Mirabella took a seat on the sofa next to Aunt Millie. She filled the two cups with the hot liquid and handed one to Aunt Millie.

"Thank you," Aunt Millie said, taking a sip and hoping that it would help to calm her at the moment.

Mirabella took the opportunity to try and explain her mixed emotions at the time of her sudden departure. She told Aunt Millie that she knew that at the time she had been a wreck mentally, emotionally and physically because she was soon dropped from several assignments. Within the first year that she had left her family she considered returning. But the longer she stayed away the more difficult it became to return. She also talked about the estrangement with her brother. Roberto had always blamed her for not really caring about their mother. Then Mirabella talked about how she met Carlos Salinas and how he had taught her everything that he knew about the advertising agency business.

"Nicole, surely you knew that once you pursued our agency, who you really are was going to come out?"

She nodded. "Yes. I think in some way I wanted it to."

"How are you planning to tell the girls that you are their mother?"

She shook her head. "I not sure, Mildred. I avoid meeting them so far, but I know I can't forever."

"Well, the people on our end have begun to wonder why you, as the buyer, haven't come to Atlanta to meet everyone."

"Yes, I know. My Sydney has been pressuring me too."

"Speaking of Sydney, is he in the office today?"

"No. He travel to our Los Angeles office this week."

"Well, I guess it's good that he's not here to see me."

Both women lifted their cup and took a long sip.

"You must know that Sydney might be falling in love with Paris," Aunt Millie stated.

Mirabella ran her fingers through her hair. "Yes, and I try to stop it from happening, but Sydney not listen to me."

"So, I take it he knows nothing about your past?"

"No."

"Well, Nicole, I don't know how you're planning to handle this whole matter, but for obvious reasons it needs to be sooner rather than later."

"Yes. I know."

"I think that the girls should know everything before this deal closes. And then let them decide what they want to do once they know the truth."

"Yes. You make good point. Maybe I talk to Sydney first, what you think?"

"Well, that's up to you, Nicole. I mean he has to know as well."

Changing the subject, Mirabella asked, "Is my brother doing well?"

Aunt Millie fished inside her purse and retrieved the white card containing the telephone number that she'd jotted down from Roberto. She handed it to Mirabella. "You need to give your brother a call, Nicole. He has something to share with you and I think you need to hear it from him."

Mirabella took the card with the number written on it. "Thank you. I will."

There was a moment of awkward silence before Mirabella spoke. "I understand from Sydney that Everson's attackers were arrested last month."

"That's true. But one was already in jail on some other charges. And I guess you also know that the other person just happened to be Paris' ex-boyfriend and the father of her six year-old son."

"Yes. Sydney explain to me everything." Mirabella's face became long as a lump formed in her throat. "Mildred, do you have picture of Paris' son?"

Aunt Millie could see the anxiousness in her eyes. Right now her own emotions were torn. Part of her wanted to understand Nicole and understand the reasons behind her actions; but another part of her wanted to rip her to shreds. Reluctantly, she pulled her wallet from her purse and opened it to the photo section. She had both a current picture of Tristan and one when he was a baby being held by Everson. She gave both to her.

As Mirabella's eyes became fixed on the photos her bottom lip began to curl. The sorrow etching her face was palpable. She ran her finger over Everson's handsome face. The joy of holding his grandson was unmistakable. Mirabella grew incurably sad as her tears began to smother her face. Instinctively, Aunt Millie moved closer and placed her arms around her. The former fashion model wept uncontrollably.

Once Mirabella had composed herself she invited Aunt Millie to have lunch with her. Aunt Millie declined, explaining to her that she had to return to Atlanta because the girls were not aware of her visit to Dallas. Aunt Millie also told her that she had no idea how the girls were going to accept the news, and that she was particularly concerned about Paris and Sydney. Mirabella said that she would hope for the best. At the very least she expected that the girls as well as Sydney would be very angry. But she realized that there was no other way. Everyone had to know the truth.

"I like to do everything over if it were possible," Mirabella said, as the two women rose from the sofa. "I make stupid mistakes at young age. I should never left family. Now I know my daughters will hate me. Possibly my son too."

Aunt Millie was unsure of how to respond. She was certain that Nicole was hurting and that she was regretful of her actions. "I don't know your religious beliefs, Nicole. But I would encourage you to pray about this."

She nodded. "That is what I do for long time now. I continue to do it."

Aunt Millie gave her another hug. "I wish things could have been different. You were married for such a short time that I didn't really get the opportunity to know you. I just knew that my brother adored you."

"Maybe future will be different."

"For everyone's sake, Nicole, I really hope so."

Mirabella stared at Aunt Millie for a moment. Then she took hold of her hands and squeezed them. "You very nice person like Everson. He too was forgiving man. All the time."

Aunt Millie smiled. "Somehow I know that if he were here instead of me, he would have found a way to forgive you."

Mirabella quickly disposed of a tear that attempted to escape her eyelids. "The girls very lucky to have you, Mildred."

Aunt Millie dismissed her accolade. "Nicole, I try and live my life with the knowledge that I will one day stand before God and give an account of my actions – good or bad. And when I do I intend to have clean hands and a pure heart. But not because of *anything* that I've done for *Him*, but because of *everything* that he's done for *me*."

Before she left Mirabella's office she gave her home telephone number and cell number to her. "I won't mention my visit to the girls," she assured her. "But I expect that you'll be making plans to visit us real soon so that this matter can be properly dealt with."

"Yes. I know what I must do," Mirabella answered. "I not young foolish woman any more."

"Nicole, what you did has nothing to do with the fact that

"you're a *woman*. More men in this world abandoned their families than women. So your behavior is *human-specific* and not *gender-specific*."

Her words proved comforting to Mirabella, invigorating her once darkened soul and bringing a glimmer of hope to her faithless heart.

CHAPTER
FORTY-FOUR

The four of them had stopped on the way from the hospital at a CHICK-FIL-A restaurant to have lunch. Tristan always enjoyed seeing the restaurant's cow mascot in the TV commercials. And last year he had the opportunity to shake hands and take a picture with the CHICK-FIL-A cow at the *LPGA's Chick-Fil-A Charity Championship* golf tournament. Paris and Milan had taken him to the event. It had been their first LPGA event and they thoroughly enjoyed their experience. The twins had discussed the possibility of having the agency participate as a sponsor within this year's event coming up in May. Although, with the acquisition deal pending, it seemed unlikely that it would happen this year.

When they stepped from the elevator onto their eighth floor lobby, Charla gave Tristan another hug before disappearing down the corridor. Other employees emerged from nearby cubicles to express their relief that the little guy hadn't been seriously injured. Milan had phoned the office earlier from the hospital to let everyone know the status of the situation.

Belinda waved in the air a stack of pink *While-You-Where-Out* message slips. She handed a stack to Milan and the rest were given to Paris. "Oh, and by the way, Paris – Naoko is waiting to see you in your office," Belinda informed her.

"How long has he been waiting?"

"Not that long."

Paris thanked her. Milan elbowed her sister and whispered

into her ear. "Remember, we can't afford to lose Naoko right now."

Paris returned to her sister a polite shove. "Well, that's not up to me," she told her. Milan smirked and then quickly scampered away. Paris asked her executive assistant to take Tristan into the break room. Some small toys were kept in one of the break room cabinets since a lot of the women at the agency also had small children who would often visit their parents at the office.

"Belinda, please hold my calls and I'll let you know when I'm finished meeting with Naoko."

"Sure," Belinda replied.

When Paris arrived at her office, Milan was just exiting. "I was simply saying hello," she told Paris as she made her way next door to her own office. Paris sucked her teeth and then closed her door. Naoko was seated on the sofa holding an envelope.

"I hope you haven't brought me another *resignation* letter," Paris remarked, placing her designer bag inside her bottom desk drawer and then joining him on the sofa.

Naoko chuckled slightly. "You sound as if you don't want me to resign."

"Of course I don't want you to resign! I told you that last week."

He handed her the envelope. "I was at home when I saw the news about the bus accident. When I heard the name of the school mentioned I knew right away that it was your son's school because you're always talking about it. I called up here and Belinda told me that you guys had already left for the hospital. She didn't know which hospital, so I decided that I at least wanted to be here when you got back. I mean I didn't know how bad things were. And I got you this card on my way here."

"Thanks, Naoko. That's very thoughtful and it really means a lot." She opened the envelope and read the card. "This is very sweet. By the way, what's with these initials *J-R-I-L-Y*?"

Naoko didn't hear her question. His eyes had suddenly become glued on the huge shiny diamond displayed prominently on Paris' finger. "Is that an engagement ring?" he asked, a wave of acid welling inside his stomach.

Paris couldn't believe that she'd forgotten to take the ring off. Of all people she did not want Naoko to see it. She attempted to play it cool. "Oh, you like it?" she asked, holding her hand in front of his face.

"Uh, yeah it looks real nice. But you didn't answer my question."

"No, it's not an engagement ring. I'm simply trying it out."

Paris could tell by his facial expression that he didn't believe her.

"That Sydney guy give it to you?"

"Okay, remember when we talked about not crossing any lines? Well, you're starting to get a little too personal, Naoko."

He threw both hands into the air in mock surrender. "Hey, I'm just asking a question. I guess I know when I've been beaten."

"What are you talking about?"

"All I know is that if one guy gives you two dozen roses and another guy gives you a three-carat diamond . . . hey, I can't compete on that level."

She considered correcting him on the carat weight but decided to let it go. "I hope you don't view me as somebody's competition because that's not what I'm about."

Naoko began stroking his chin. "I don't view you like that, Paris. But I know that some women get easily impressed by all the Bling-Bling."

She couldn't believe that he would sit here and insult her. "Have you forgotten that I am a co-owner of this multi-million dollar agency? Do I really look like I need anybody's Bling?"

He attempted to back down. "I'm not trying to upset you."

"And you haven't. But I don't appreciate you insinuating that Sydney, you or anyone else can buy my love. Because for that to be true my love would have to be for sale. And let me tell you something – that's one for sale sign that I've never worn and will never wear."

Naoko bit his bottom lip. "Yeah, I hear you."

"Now, let's keep the remainder of this conversation on a professional level."

The two of them talked for another half-hour. They discussed whether or not he really wanted to remain with the ad agency. Paris made it clear that she would not beg him to

188 / CORNELL GRAHAM

stay. She and Milan both wanted him to stay. But if he insisted on leaving then they would respect his decision. Naoko also came clean and admitted that he did want to remain at the agency, but that at the moment he needed some time to deal with the feelings that he'd developed for her. Paris did not want to appear insensitive, so she suggested that he take some time off – as much as he needed – to work through his feelings. She assured him that his job would be waiting for him when he returned.

"I really appreciate your understanding, Paris. And I don't think that I'll need that much time off – maybe a couple of weeks."

"Oh, so is that all the time it takes for you to forget about me?" she joked.

He laughed. "I wish."

"You're a good man, Naoko. The right woman is out there somewhere."

"Humph. Yeah, somewhere."

After Naoko had left her office Paris buzzed her sister and shared with her what they had agreed upon. Milan was okay with it. She was just glad that someone as talented as Naoko would not be leaving them for one of their rivals.

CHAPTER
FORTY-FIVE

Traffic from the airport was congested as Aunt Millie made her way home. She had phoned Blade Barnes from Dallas and asked him to meet her at her house this evening. His schedule was clear so he agreed to do so. Blade had asked what the meeting was about and Aunt Millie told him that she did not want to get into it over the phone, but that it was of the utmost importance. She also asked him not to mention their meeting to either Milan or Paris.

During her phone conversation with Blade he informed her about the school bus accident, which almost sent her into a panic attack. She was relieved when Blade told her that Tristan had been picked up from the hospital and had not suffered any real injuries other than a small scratch on the forehead. Still, Aunt Millie felt guilty for not being there. She was certain that the girls must have been trying to reach her, although there were no calls from either of them on her cell.

It was nearing six o'clock as she drove through the downtown area. Her meeting with Blade had been scheduled for seven. She decided to give Paris a call just to check in. Paris' voice-mail answered at the office so she tried her cell phone.

"Hi, Paris," Aunt Millie said when Paris answered.

"Aunt Millie! Where are you? Milan and I have been calling the house all day! Tristan and I are on our way to your house now."

"Um, I'm in the car right now. Actually, I won't be home for at least another two hours," she lied. "I heard about the accident and I wanted to make sure that everything was okay."

"Yeah, Tristan is fine. Once we left the hospital I decided to keep him with me at the office. Aunt Millie are you okay?"

"Sure! I'm fine. I apologize that I couldn't be at the hospital with you, but I took some flu medication earlier this morning and I have been out of it all day. And I had the ringer on the phones turned off so I didn't wake until just recently. I'm taking care of some errands right now."

Paris detected that her aunt didn't sound like she'd been sick or even groggy from the medication. "Well, I'm glad that you're feeling better."

Aunt Millie asked to speak with Tristan a moment. Tristan couldn't wait to tell his accident story again. This time a big truck had *smashed* him. Aunt Millie told him how proud she was of him for handling everything so well. When Paris returned to the phone she told her that she was going to give Milan a call.

"Aunt Millie," Paris began before the call ended.

"Yes, honey?"

"I have some good news to tell you about later."

"Oh, really?" Aunt Millie responded. "What kind of good news?"

"Well, I have something to *show* you, so I'm not saying anything over the phone."

Aunt Millie paused, wondering what she could be talking about. "Then I guess I'll have to wait until I see you, huh?"

"That's right."

When their call ended it occurred to Aunt Millie that Paris' good news might have something to do with Sydney. A snarl of anxiety began to spread over her face. It had been quite awhile since she'd seen Paris so happy. Whatever *good* news her niece was going to share with her, it was bound to be overwhelmed by the *bad* news that was about to be shared by *Mirabella Nicole Salinas*.

CHAPTER
FORTY-SIX

Cobalt blue was the special color that Blade Barnes had chosen for his Range Rover. He noticed Mildred standing in the doorway when he drove the vehicle into her driveway. *This must really be important*, he thought to himself.

The evening air had become increasingly cool, but all the rain had dissipated from the area. Blade rarely wore a coat despite the temperature. He was clad in his two-piece tailor-made suit as he walked to her door.

"Good evening, Mildred," he spoke as he arrived at the front door.

"Hello, Blade. I appreciate you coming by."

Aunt Millie welcomed him inside. She offered him a seat in the den. He sat in a cream-colored leather recliner. "You have a very lovely home," he complimented her, taking note of how warm and cozy the home felt.

"Thank you. Can I get you something to drink?"

Blade thought for a moment. "Uh, what do you have?"

"Pretty much everything – water, soda, coffee, tea. Except alcohol, of course. I'm not a drinker."

Blade flashed her a smile. "Good for you. A hot cup of tea will be just fine."

"Caffeine or decaf?"

"Decaf, please."

"I have a variety of flavors – *Earl Grey, Constant Comment, Mango Orange* . . ."

"Surprise me," he told her.

Minutes later Aunt Millie returned with a cup of Earl Grey tea. She handed it to him and then sat in the other matching recliner.

"So, what's on your mind?" Blade asked, anxious to learn what was going on.

Aunt Millie had chosen a Lipton Brisk Iced Tea in the can as her beverage. A straw protruded from the can. She took a sip. "Well, I really don't quite know how to begin."

Blade remained silent as he allowed her time to gather her thoughts.

"Earlier this morning I left a voice-mail message at the office for Milan telling her that I was not feeling well and would not be in the office today."

Blade's eyebrows furrowed deeply.

She continued, "But actually, I wasn't telling the truth. Basically, I didn't want either of the girls to know that I was taking a trip to Dallas this morning." She watched his eyebrows shift, shooting up in surprise.

"Dallas?"

Aunt Millie nodded. "I went to see Mirabella Salinas."

Blade shifted his position in the chair and set down his teacup on the coffee table. "I'm sure you're going to tell me why?"

Aunt Millie retrieved a manila folder that she had setting on the end table. She opened it and pulled out the ADWEEK article and handed it to Blade. "This is a feature that was written about Mirabella a couple of weeks ago. I want you to take a good look at the two photos of her and tell me what you think."

Blade studied the two photos within the article. "Well, it's safe to say that the woman's beauty is ageless. How much age difference is there between the two photos?"

"One is current and the other is at least twenty years old."

Blade began shaking his head. "Wow. I had no idea that she used to be a fashion model."

"Look carefully at the older picture, Blade. Doesn't she resemble *someone* we know?"

Blade squinted his eyes, scrutinizing the photo even more. "I got nothing, Mildred. Other than the fact that she is a very "beautiful woman. I mean should I *recognize* her?"

Aunt Millie was about to answer him when it suddenly occurred to her that Blade had never seen Nicole. What was she thinking? She erroneously assumed that since he'd always been her brother's attorney that he'd met Nicole. But now that she thought about it, Nicole had been gone long before Blade met Everson through a law firm that he once worked for. She shook her head, trying to regain her thoughts.

"Actually, Blade, you're not going to recognize her. But I will tell you who she is."

Blade looked perplexed. "Barring the fact that I haven't formally met her, Mildred, I do know who she is."

"No, you don't understand what I mean," Aunt Millie began to explain. She took the article away from Blade and held it up. "This woman – Mirabella Salinas – is also Mirabella Nicole Alexander."

It took a moment for her words to sink in. "Alexander?" Blade repeated, in almost a whisper. "What are you saying, Mildred?"

"Blade, this woman is also Milan's and Paris' mother. My brother's ex-wife! My former sister-in-law!"

"Mildred, no!"

"Believe me, I wish it were not true."

Blade's lean body sunk deeper into the chair as he exhaled towards the ceiling. "Are you certain? I mean . . . how did you . . . when . . .?" The questions were escaping his mouth before he could even complete them.

Aunt Millie then explained everything to him, including her conversation this past weekend with Nicole's brother. When she was finished, Blade was totally blown away by it all.

"Wow!" he said for the second time. "This is all unbelievable! Does she realize the effect this news is going to have on everyone involved?"

"You know, I'm really not sure that she does. I mean the relationship between Paris and Sydney alone is going to have major implications."

"Man oh man. I didn't even consider that. From what Milan tells me those two have gotten very close to one another."

Aunt Millie nodded. "They're pretty serious."

"So, what's next? I mean do we just sit and wait for her to

"make her next move or what?"

"Well, Blade, I explained to Nicole that this whole matter has to be dealt with sooner rather than later, and she understands that. I think for the time being we cannot say anything to the girls about this. I mean this sort of thing has to come from Nicole."

Blade agreed. "What about the acquisition?"

"Well, she wanted me to see if you can stall things on our end. After all, once the truth about who she is comes out, we have no idea how the girls are going to react – or even Sydney for that matter."

Blade picked up his teacup from the coffee table and took another sip. "You know, Milan and I were just talking the other day about the series of events that have taken place over the last year – the hostage ordeal, the arrest of Scotty Sims – and she wondered if there was another shoe out there somewhere just waiting to drop."

"Well, unfortunately there is. And there's no denying that based on the *size* of this particular shoe, it's going to be one heck of a drop."

CHAPTER
FORTY-SEVEN

Tristan had already been tucked snugly beneath the covers of his bed when Paris decided to drive over to her aunt's house. It was almost nine o'clock. She'd phoned Milan earlier and asked her to meet her at Aunt Millie's as well.

Before leaving her townhouse she gave Tristan another peck on the cheek. She could tell that he was tired because he barely moved a muscle when she kissed him. "Night mommy," he uttered, nearly asleep. She would decide in the morning whether or not to keep him home from school. Of course, now was as good a time as any to take him out of THORNHILL CHRISTIAN ACADEMY and enroll him in the public elementary school that was just down the street. She knew several parents whose children were enrolled in North Fulton County's public school system and they were all doing quite well. Not having to receive another phone call from that nagging Miss Montgomery was motivation alone.

Paris told Nikki that she shouldn't be gone too long. Nikki already knew about the engagement ring and had expressed her sentiments with enthusiasm. She told Paris that if anyone deserved love and happiness it was she. Paris thanked her and gave her a heart-felt hug before walking out the door.

Both their cars arrived at Aunt Millie's house at the same time. Milan and Paris parked beside one another in the driveway.

"Hey girl," Paris greeted her sister upon exiting the car.

"Hi, Sis," Milan returned the greeting. They hugged one another before walking up to the door.

"Are you sure you want to drop this news on Aunt Millie tonight?" Milan asked.

"Well, you know we tell Aunt Millie everything. She'd be hurt if she found out from some loud mouth at the office."

Milan looked surprised. "Just how many people at the office know already?"

"Belinda!" Paris answered, chuckling.

Milan couldn't restrain her own laugh. "Telling Belinda is like plastering the news on a billboard in the middle of Buckhead!"

They laughed some more.

Before they could ring the doorbell the door opened. "What are you two doing out here laughing like hyenas?" Aunt Millie scolded them in teasing fashion.

"Hey, Aunt Millie," Paris spoke first as she gave her aunt a hug. Milan greeted her as well and hugged her tightly.

"We missed you at the office today," Milan told her.

"I know. I'm sorry that I had to be out."

"Paris said that you had the flu."

"Well, I thought it was the flu. After taking some medication, I feel much better. The flu usually takes much longer to get over."

The three of them headed straight for the kitchen where they sat at the kitchen table. "Are you girls hungry? Can I get you anything?"

Both declined. "We're not going to stay too long, Aunt Millie," Milan stated. "Paris just wanted to share some good news with you."

Aunt Millie had almost forgotten about her earlier conversation with Paris. "Oh, that's right, Paris. Well, don't keep me in suspense any longer. Tell me what's this big news you got!"

Paris had been shielding her left hand from her aunt's view. Now, while sitting at the kitchen table, her left hand was tucked behind her back. Aunt Millie directed her attention towards her niece. Milan held her breath. Then slowly, Paris brought her hand forward and set it on the table, the TIFFANY diamond ring glistened in full view.

As Aunt Millie stared at the jewel a dull, empty ache began to gnaw at her. Suddenly her throat was constricted and her chest grew heavy.

"Well, Aunt Millie – you like?" Paris asked, anxious for a response – any response.

She cleared her throat and placed her hand over her chest to take a deep breath. "Well, it's beautiful. Need I ask what it is?"

Without hesitation Paris replied, "It's an engagement ring from Sydney."

Aunt Millie had already assumed as much. "An engagement ring? Goodness, aren't you two moving a little too fast? When did he give it to you?"

Paris held her hand up towards the light and gazed dreamily at the ring. "He proposed on Valentine's Day."

"And you accepted?"

"Well, not at first. He gave me time to think it over. But I've thought it over, Aunt Millie. When he gets back from L.A. I'm going to tell him that my answer is *yes!*"

Aunt Millie glanced at Milan. "What do you think about all this?"

Milan shrugged her shoulders. She realized that her sister had asked for her presence this evening for moral support. And while she wasn't all that crazy about the whole engagement thing, she knew that she had to provide support for Paris. "Aunt Millie, I've always wanted my sister to be happy, in every way possible. And if this is what she wants then I'm happy for her."

Paris fought back a tear. "Thank you, girl," she told Milan.

Aunt Millie also wanted desperately to be supportive. But knowing what she knew it was very difficult for her to express support to her niece at the moment. "Of course I want you to be happy as well, Paris. It's just that, well, you and Sydney haven't known each other for very long. And that concerns me."

Paris reached across the table and grabbed her aunt's hand. "Aunt Millie, all I can tell you is that it feels so right! No one has ever made me feel the way Sydney does. Some things you just know, and *this* I know."

"Sydney's a really nice guy," Milan weighed in.

"Of course he is," Aunt Millie said. "I'm not doubting that at all. It just that . . . well, there's a lot going on right now and I just think that maybe you two should put personal feelings aside until everything's sorted out."

"Are you referring to the acquisition?" Paris asked.

Aunt Millie hesitated before speaking. "Yes. This acquisition by Sydney's agency is going to put you two on a different level. Wouldn't you want to wait and see what impact that's going to have?"

Milan realized that everything her aunt was saying made sense. And she hoped that her sister was allowing it to sink in. "Hey, it's not like Paris is getting married tomorrow, right? So, let's not get all worked up about it."

Paris cut her eyes sharply at her sister. "Maybe *not* tomorrow, but I'm not planning to wait a long time either."

Aunt Millie couldn't listen to any more of the current conversation. She quickly changed the subject, asking Paris to bring her up to date on the construction of her new home. Their chatter continued until almost eleven o'clock. And since they all had to be at work tomorrow morning, the night was brought to a close. She stood at the front entrance of her house and watched Milan and Paris get into their cars. As they each pulled from the driveway, Aunt Millie waved goodbye, unable to escape the feeling that an ominous dark cloud was looming over the heads of her dearly beloved nieces.

CHAPTER
FORTY-EIGHT

"Sweetheart, did I awake you?" Sydney asked when Paris answered the telephone on the fourth ring. He'd forgotten that Los Angeles' time was three hours behind that of Atlanta's.

Paris was wide-awake, though it was just past midnight. "Hi there!" she said cheerfully. "I was hoping I'd hear from you tonight."

Just the sound of her voice warmed him immensely. "I missed you."

"And I you!"

"So, how was your day?"

"Considering how it started, it turned out to be a good day." She then told him about Tristan's school bus accident. He expressed genuine concern, but was relieved that Tristan hadn't been hurt and was doing okay. Sydney also told Paris that he was sorry he wasn't there for her, but she assured him that an apology wasn't even necessary. Everything had worked out fine.

"Guess what?" she said.

"Now, you know that I'm no good at this game!"

She chuckled. "Yeah, that's right. I do beat you at every game we play don't I?"

He took offense. "Hey, I wouldn't go that far!"

"It's true!" she said, laughing heartily. "Anyway, tonight I told my aunt about our engagement!"

"Really? So, does that you mean you've accepted?"

"Oh, I meant to tell you that – the answer is yes!"

Sydney let out an enormous yell that continued for several seconds. It sounded as if he'd just won the lottery.

"Are you jumping up and down on the bed?" Paris asked.

"Not anymore!" he answered.

"You are so silly!"

"I love you Paris Alexander! And I want the whole world to know it!"

She heard more shouts from him.

"Okay, let's calm down. I'm sure everyone in your hotel doesn't care to know how you feel about me."

"But I care!"

After more celebratory shouts, Sydney regained his composure.

"You haven't been drinking have you?" she teased.

"Sweetheart, if I'm inebriated it's from your love!"

"You are the sweetest, Sydney."

He asked her how her aunt responded to the news and Paris went on to tell him about the night with Aunt Millie and Milan.

"Well, it sounds as if she's not terribly upset," he said.

"Of course not! Aunt Millie is very supportive."

"Well, I can only hope for the same from my mother."

"You think she won't approve of me?"

"No, it's not that. It just might take her awhile to come around. I mean I am her first-born and her only child."

"Yeah, I guess that would be hard for a mother."

Sydney told her that he would be finished with his tasks in L.A. by Wednesday. He'd decided that he was going to have his mother meet him in Atlanta and then the two of them could break the news to her together. Paris thought it was a good idea. She was really looking forward to meeting his mother.

"Well, I won't keep you up any longer, my love," he said.

"Why? You think I need my beauty sleep?"

He chuckled. "Sweetheart, no amount of sleep could possibly enhance your beauty."

"Okay, you're making me blush way too much! Goodnight, Sydney Salinas!"

"Goodnight, Paris *Salinas*."

CHAPTER
FORTY-NINE

Tossing and turning had become too much for Aunt Millie. She simply couldn't go to sleep. She glanced over at her clock on the nightstand. It was 12:30 A.M. She decided that she couldn't wait any longer. Sitting up in bed she grabbed the telephone and called Nicole. When she answered on the other end, Aunt Millie apologized.

"I know it's late, Nicole, but I just couldn't wait until morning."

Mirabella had been sitting in a chair in her bedroom staring out the window at a starless sky. "Don't worry," she told Aunt Millie. "I not go to sleep anytime soon."

"Well, I don't know how to tell you this, but the girls came over to my house tonight and . . . well, Sydney has given Paris an engagement ring."

Mirabella was silent.

"Are you still there?"

"Yes," she answered. "My worst nightmare comes true."

"Well, nothing has happened yet," Aunt Millie said, attempting to minimize the news.

"I just get off telephone with my son minutes ago. He tell me to meet him in Atlanta on Thursday."

"Did he mention the engagement?"

"No. He only say that he has good news to share."

Aunt Millie began gathering her thoughts. "Nicole, that has to be the time to tell them."

"I know you are right, Mildred. But what I tell him will break his heart."

"It probably will, Nicole. But you'll also be stopping him from making a serious mistake. And neither us know how the girls are going to react."

"My girls will hate me even more."

Aunt Millie could hear Nicole's sniffles. "At first, undoubtedly, they probably will be very angry at you. But I know that neither Milan nor Paris can harbor hatred in their hearts."

"I guess you know them better."

"Nicole, I am very much in prayer about this. You can only control the things that you're going to say to them. You cannot control how they're going to react."

"I know."

"So, are you going to come on Thursday?"

"I have no choice."

"Well, you're welcome to stay at my house."

"Thank you, Mildred. But I stay in hotel. Same hotel I stay in when I come to Everson's funeral."

"You were at the funeral?" Aunt Millie asked, surprised.

"Yes. I sit in back of church. I wear big hat and dark glasses. No one notice me. But I had to say goodbye to him."

"Well, it's good to know that you came, Nicole."

"I only wish I never leave."

"Well, none of us can undo the past."

Mirabella went on to get the directions to the ALEXANDER AGENCY offices. She told Aunt Millie that she would be flying in on Thursday morning on their corporate jet and that she would be staying at the RITZ-CARLTON in Buckhead.

"Nicole," Aunt Millie began. "I forgive you for what you did to my brother and to my nieces. But if you're going to get through this ordeal you have to also forgive yourself."

With her voice cracking, Mirabella thanked Aunt Millie and hung up the telephone. She would eventually fall asleep in the chair that was adjacent to her bed. The only light penetrating the room came from the moon, which had cast a salient glow over the pensive face of Mirabella Salinas as she lay sleeping.

CHAPTER
FIFTY

Thursday, FEBRUARY 19, 2004 would become a day that would stay etched in their memories for many years. Not for the record-high temperature that was being forecast, though it was going to be a beautiful Spring-like day. Nor for the exciting news that the FEDERAL RESERVE was going to lower the interest rate. The significance of this particular day lie in the revelation that was about to be made known to three unsuspecting individuals whose lives will be impacted beyond measure.

At 9:30 A.M. it was so far a typical busy morning at the offices of the ALEXANDER AGENCY. An hour earlier, the sleek corporate jet carrying Mirabella Salinas made a smooth landing at Atlanta's Peachtree-DeKalb Airport. As the waiting limousine drove her to the RITZ-CARLTON hotel in the Buckhead area of Atlanta, she quickly realized that the rest of her day would be anything but smooth.

Sydney Salinas had arrived in Atlanta last night from Los Angeles. He'd overslept this morning. Paris had just left the office to pick him up from his WESTIN HOTEL at the Perimeter Mall. His mother phoned him from the limo moments ago to let him know that she would be at the agency's offices by eleven o'clock. He hadn't seen her since he left Dallas on Monday for L.A., so he told her that he was anxious to see her. She had savored his words, knowing just how fleeting they may soon become.

Aunt Millie paced back and forth inside her office, unable to concentrate on anything other than what was about to occur. Her hands were shaking so badly that she spilled hot tea on herself when she'd tried to hold the cup. With her voice cracking she told Belinda to hold all of her calls for now.

The main conference room had been chosen as the place where they would all meet. Milan and Paris assumed it to be a business meeting where they would finally meet Mirabella Salinas. Sydney assumed likewise, although he and Paris had also chosen the moment to reveal their own surprise.

Blade was present in the conference room, which delighted Milan, but she couldn't help wondering why the other members of their specially appointed acquisition team were not present. Blade brushed off her concern, telling her that they had another meeting scheduled with Mirabella later that afternoon at his office.

At 10:50 A.M., seated around the large conference table were just the five of them – Blade, Aunt Millie, Milan, Paris and Sydney. The seat at the head of the conference table was left noticeably vacant. Opposite the head chair on one side of the table sat Aunt Millie, Milan and then Blade. On the other side is where Paris and Sydney nestled. A serving tray containing hot tea, coffee and orange juice had been brought in.

Nervous chatter filled the room – Aunt Millie and Blade were more nervous than the others even realized. Paris and Sydney were locked at the arms and they were holding hands. The diamond ring on her finger seemed to be shining even brighter.

Having learned of the engagement on Tuesday from Aunt Millie, Blade couldn't help but feel sadness for the two of them. He knew that this news was going to devastate their worlds.

"Why don't I give my mother a call on her cell and see what's keeping her," Sydney spoke, after glancing at his watch and seeing that it was a minute before eleven. But then the telephone in the room buzzed. It was Belinda announcing that Mirabella Salinas had just stepped off the elevator. Milan told her to have one of their executive assistants escort her to the conference room.

Other than the exterior windows, the main conference room did not have a typical glass wall that could be found in many conference room facilities. So none of them had the pleasure of seeing Mirabella until the executive assistant had opened the door and showed Mirabella inside.

Undoubtedly, she was a towering figure of beauty. A two-piece navy suit adorned her lean frame. Her long jet-black hair stretched well beyond her shoulders. A pair of dark sunglasses shielded her eyes. She was not carrying any sort of attaché case, only the *Jessica Simpson*-type LOUIS VUITTON bag hung from her arm.

Both Sydney and Blade stood from the table upon her entrance into the room. Sydney rushed over and welcomed his mother, giving her a warm embrace. Milan thanked the executive assistant as she departed from the room, closing the door behind her.

Sydney proceeded to introduce her. He began with Blade, then Aunt Millie, followed by Milan and finally, Paris. Mirabella shook hands with each of them. Paris was careful to extend the hand without the ring.

"I finally meet you all," she said as Sydney led her to the chair at the head of the table. She removed her sunglasses and placed them inside her bag. She made herself comfortable in the chair, placing her bag on the floor.

"Did you have a good flight?" Milan asked.

She looked at the beautiful young woman sitting across the table. She had to muster up every ounce of strength to maintain her composure. "Yes, the flight here very good," she answered. She stole a glance at Paris – their eyes met. Mirabella flashed a nervous smile.

Aunt Millie's heart was pounding so loudly that she was certain everyone else could hear its beating. Despite the brilliance from the sunshine outside the conference room windows, this bleak, wintry feeling overwhelmed her.

Realizing that the other shoe was about to drop, Blade took Milan's hand in his and held it ever so tightly, like they were kids who were preparing to ride a roller coaster for the very first time. She turned toward him and winked salaciously.

Sensing that there didn't appear to be any set agenda for the *business* meeting, Sydney spoke, "Uh, mother, perhaps "you'd like Blade and I to give a status report as to how we're coming along with the acquisition?"

Before Blade could say anything Mirabella quickly spoke. "No, Sydney. Status report not necessary at moment." She paused, surveying each of their faces. "My presence here today is not business. I have something important to share. You will not like what I have to say. But the time has come."

Sydney's face became tight, pinched. Milan and Paris exchanged glances. Both were thinking that Mirabella was about to call off her plans to acquire their ad agency.

"Forgive me if I not as forthcoming as I should be, but this very difficult for me."

Sydney was now very concerned. "Mother, is something wrong?"

She held up her hand. "Son, please. Let me get through this."

Sydney held his tongue.

Mirabella continued to speak, quite often not knowing what words would emanate from her mouth. "As young girl, I always look at fashion magazines. I tell myself I would become top model one day. I go to college like my mother wanted, but I drop out after one year to pursue my dream. Modeling." The more she spoke the more it seemed that blood drained from her face, which was quickly becoming pale, ashen.

"One day I get call from New York modeling agency. They sign me to contract. Right away I get international assignment to travel first to Italy and then France. It was dream come true. But, while I away my mother died. My life become very sad then. I not want to model any more. Just come home. To Florida. But my brother, he very angry. He blame me for breaking our mother's heart. I move away. Come to Atlanta. Start modeling again. In Atlanta I meet handsome man. Nice man. He love me very much. I love him too. We get married. But I still not happy. Life still so sad for me."

"Mother, why are saying these things," Sydney interrupted.

She ignored his question. "We not married for long time. Soon I pregnant with baby." She paused and then uttered softly, "*Two* babies. Twin girls."

Milan was the first to consider where the conversation was

heading. But it didn't take long for Paris to make the connection as well. The two sisters stared at one another from across the table, eyes widening in alarm. Sydney was still trying to make sense of his mother's speaking.

"What are you trying to say, Mirabella?" Milan asked nervously.

By now, Mirabella could barely focus on anyone within the room because her eyes had welled over with tears. "I once married to your father," her voice quavered as she looked at both the twins. "I am your mother!"

Like a brick thrown into the river, Mirabella's head dropped suddenly to the table as shrill cries erupted from her.

Milan, Paris and Sydney each sat motionless. Aunt Millie was fighting a losing battle against her own tears. And Blade had wrapped both his arms around Milan, who now had buried her head into his chest. Paris and Sydney were still clutching hands before they instinctively pulled back. The twins looked at their aunt, her pained expression spoke volumes to them.

"Aunt Millie, did you know?" Paris asked, confusion still masking her face.

"Mildred just learned of my identity on Monday," Mirabella spoke ahead of Aunt Millie.

Aunt Millie then told the girls that she told Blade that same evening but did not want to be the one to tell them.

Sydney stood from the table, his nostrils flaring. "How could you do this, mother? Do you realize what you've done!"

"Sydney, I try and stop you! But you fall in love anyway."

"Don't you dare try and put this on me! You've known all these years that Milan and Paris were your daughters and you said nothing! Why did you make me the one to come to Atlanta, mother? Was I supposed to somehow magically discover that they were my sisters!"

As Sydney yelled, Paris felt empty inside. She could feel the walls closing in on her. Her face was flush and she felt incredibly sick to her stomach. She tore herself from the table and bolted from the room.

"Paris, wait!" Aunt Millie called after her. But Paris sprinted down the corridor. She burst through her office door, slamming it behind her. And like a rag doll her body crumpled

208 / CORNELL GRAHAM

to the floor as she curled into the fetal position.

Milan broke away from Blade's arms. "I'm going to check on my sister," she said. Before exiting the conference room she turned and glared at Mirabella. "I guess hurting us for twenty-six years wasn't enough for you?" she told her before storming out the door.

Sydney was the next to remove himself from the table. He walked over and stood before his mother. "Look at me, mother!" he demanded.

Mirabella turned her tear-drenched, stricken face towards her son. She'd never seen such hurt and anger in his eyes before. She was writhing in pain. But at the moment Sydney could care less about his mother's feelings. "You chose to walk away from your own daughters, mother. Remain absent from their lives for twenty-six years! That's absolutely unforgivable!"

"Sydney, I make big mistake!" she cried, reaching for his hand.

He snatched it away from her grasp. "Don't touch me!" he yelled. "What kind of mother are you? I don't even know you anymore!"

"Sydney, please!" she begged.

He turned from her and began walking towards the door.

Mirabella screamed louder. "Sydney, don't go!"

He stopped, his back still towards her.

"Please, stay!" she cried out.

He turned around and said, "You walked away from your daughters, and now I'm walking away from you!"

CHAPTER
FIFTY-ONE

Three weeks had gone by since the revelation. Milan and Paris were still trying to come to terms with it all. Both had taken leave of absences from the ad agency. Aunt Millie told them that it was probably a good decision. And since they had no idea how long they would be away, Blade appointed two of the agency's senior managers to oversee day-to-day operations during the interim. The acquisition by SALINAS WORLDWIDE was on hold, although not altogether dead.

When the news became public that Mirabella Salinas was the birth mother of Milan and Paris, a media frenzy ensued. The twins, however, stayed away from all media interview requests – print, radio and television. Most people were sympathetic to their plight, however. And as time moved along, they began to respect their privacy with regards to the entire matter.

It was a warm and beautiful day in March. Milan and Paris were sitting in Paris' den contemplating their future. Lately, Aunt Millie had been serving as a liaison between them and Mirabella. They had learned a lot about their mother over the past three weeks. They'd also learned about the uncle they never knew they had.

"So, have you heard anything from Sydney?" Milan was curious.

Paris shook her head. "No. Aunt Millie says that his mother hasn't heard from him either."

"Well, he was visibly upset when he left that day," Milan said.

"Yeah, weren't we all!"

"That's true. I guess he just needs time to heal as well."

Paris brushed a strand of hair from her face. "Milan, how does a person move from being engaged to the love of their life one minute, to finding out that the person is their brother the next minute?"

Milan moved closer on the sofa to her sister. She put an arm around her shoulder. "It'll take some time, Paris. Neither of you guys knew. But, no matter what I will always be right here for you."

"Thanks, Milan," Paris said, returning a gentle hug to her sister.

"Can you believe it though? Finding out that we have a brother and having our mother revealed to us all in the same day?"

"Yeah, at the same time!" Paris remarked.

Aunt Millie would share with the twins whatever additional information Mirabella chose to share with her. The girls had learned how they got their names. Since their mother's first modeling assignment had been in *Milan, Italy* and since Milan was the first of the twins to be born, she was given that name. Their mother's second assignment was in *Paris, France* and so *Paris* was the name given to the other twin. Mirabella's last international modeling assignment had been in *Sydney, Australia* and when she gave birth to a son a few years later, she gave him the name Sydney.

While they were talking the doorbell rang. Paris rose from the sofa and headed towards the front door. She wondered who it could be – Tristan was at school and Nikki had gone shopping. Besides, Nikki has her own key.

"Hi there!" Naoko greeted her when she opened the door.

Paris hadn't seen him nor talked to him since their last meeting at the office early last month. "Hey, Naoko! What are you doing here?"

"Oh, just thought I'd stop by and see how you doing," he answered, a wide grin spreading across his face.

"I'm doing okay, I guess," she told him. She invited him inside. "Milan and I was just sitting around chatting."

When he arrived in the den he greeted Milan. They exchanged hugs. Sensing that Naoko might want some one-on-one time with her sister, Milan told Paris that she needed to leave.

"Please don't leave on my account," Naoko told Milan.

She fanned the air with her hand. "Not at all! I'm supposed to meet Blade for lunch so I need to run home and change."

"Thanks so much for coming over," Paris told Milan, giving her a hug before she left. Naoko remained in the den while Paris walked her sister to the door.

Moments later Paris returned to the den.

"Everyone misses you at the office," Naoko stated.

Paris nodded. "I know. But I'm not ready to go back."

Naoko considered his words before speaking again. "Paris, I know that you have a lot to deal with, but I really want you to know that I'll do whatever I can to help you get through this."

She smiled. "Isn't life funny?"

"What do you mean?"

"I mean all the time while I was I looking at Sydney as my Knight in shining armor, you seemed to somehow always be right there as well."

"Nothing's changed on my end, Paris."

"You're a good person, Naoko. I cannot believe no one has captured your heart!"

He blushed. "Someone has."

She smiled again. "I have a mother in my life now and a brother – neither of whom I can talk to right now."

"That's understandable."

Paris did not want to break into tears in front of Naoko – she was still his boss. But her feeble emotions were starting to get the better of her. She turned away from him.

Naoko could see that she was fighting back tears. He got up from the chair and moved next to her on the sofa. "Everything will be all right, Paris."

She dried her eyes with the back of her hand. "I wish I knew that to be true."

"It's hard to believe right now, but trust me it will be all right."

She rubbed his shoulder. "Thanks for saying that."

"Hey, I'm not just saying it. I believe it."

Paris leaned over and kissed him on the cheek.

"You didn't have to do that."

"I know."

Naoko took his hand and brushed away several strands of hair from her face. "J-RILY," he said to her.

"Okay, what's the deal with this *J-RILY!* Every card you've ever given me has had those initials at the bottom! What's up with that, Naoko?"

It was his turn to smile. "Wait a minute, all right?" he said, excusing himself and dashing out to his car. When he returned he held a CD in his hand. He asked if she had a CD player. She pointed to it across the room. Naoko walked over and popped the disk into the player. Before he pressed the play button he said, "The initials J-R-I-L-Y are from the title of one of my favorite songs – *Just Remember I Love You* – recorded by *Firefall*."

The song began to play.

When it all goes crazy and the thrill is gone
The days get rainy and the nights get long
When you get that feelin' you were born to lose
Staring at your ceiling thinkin' of your blues

When there's so much trouble that you wanna cry
The world has crumbled and you don't know why
When your hopes are fading and they can't be found
Dreams have left you waiting, friends have let you down

Just remember I love you
And it'll be alright
Just remember I love you
More than I can say . . .

By the time the song ended Paris' face was bathed in tears and Naoko was doing a poor job of keeping his moistening eyes dry as well.

"I don't know what to say, Naoko," Paris spoke in a whispering voice.

"There's nothing you need to say. Just don't ever forget those five letters."

EPILOGUE

Spring had settled in quite nicely by the middle of May. A week earlier Milan and Paris had flown to Dallas to have dinner with their mother to celebrate Mother's Day. Tristan stayed behind with Aunt Millie. Paris first wanted to build her relationship with her mother before she brought Tristan into the mix. Sydney had also been present at their mother's home in *Flower Mound, Texas* and so had been Roberto, his wife and their two sons.

All things considered, the somber holiday had gone quite well. The twins had already begun speaking to their mother with frequent telephone calls. Sydney had returned home by the end of March. Apparently he'd gone to stay with an old college friend of his to clear his head. Upon his return he'd called Paris. They enjoyed a lengthy conversation. Both realized the difficulty that they faced in trying to *rearrange* their feelings, but each was committed to doing just that. But Roberto's future outlook was not so positive.

The twins had returned to work on May 3rd. It had been agreed that they would continue with the acquisition of their agency by their mother's agency. The deal was set to close on June 20th – Father's Day – in honor and memory of Everson Alexander.

Milan and Blade were growing closer in their relationship. He secretly shared with Paris that he was thinking about proposing to her sister before the end of summer.

Milan, however, didn't talk much about her relationship with Blade out of respect for her sister, who was still resisting the more obvious and forward advances of Naoko Jackson.

On this Wednesday afternoon, Milan and Paris were resting, seated on a bench outside the GUCCI store at PHIPPS PLAZA. They had decided to spend their lunchtime doing some shopping.

"Paris, are your feelings about our mom changing each day?" Milan was curious.

Paris shrugged her shoulders as she sipped on a SPRITE. "Maybe a little each day now," she answered.

"I guess mine are too," Milan said.

"She seems remorseful about everything," Paris added.

"I know. And she's really nice, so it's kind of hard to hate her."

"Well, I never *hated* her," Paris quickly interjected.

Milan shook her head. "Wrong choice of words. But you know, Paris – I'm beginning to think that maybe one day we will all be one big happy family!"

"Yeah, well, I guess time will tell."

"It sure will. And like they say, *time can heal all wounds.*"

Paris thought for a moment. "Yeah, but the *scars* left behind can last a lifetime."

MAYBE

Maybe there's a song that tells how I feel
Where the melody and all the words are real

And maybe there's a line that says what I need
Or one that says without you I can't breathe

Maybe through the lines you'll know what is true
'Cause this ol' heart is aching just for you

So let me go to try and search
To heal this love and heal this hurt, we choose
I know your pain, your agony
And I need your truth your honesty, or lose

Maybe, sometimes I think just maybe
You will wait for me
Maybe, sometimes I think just maybe
Your love will set me free

Maybe there's a place where I can go and hide
Where you can't see the tears that fill my eyes

Maybe there's a mask to cover up my face
Conceal the lines your fingers used to trace

Maybe there's a bitter pill that I can take
To forget about the sorrows I feel awake

I know a man ain't supposed to cry
But whatever it takes I will try, for you
Just give me a chance to love you right
Find my way back to the light, that's true

Maybe, sometimes I think just maybe
You will wait for me
Maybe, sometimes I think just maybe
Your love will set me free

– Cornell Graham